Praise For Karl Di

"Drinkwater creates fantastically believable characters."

On The Shelf Reviews

"Each book remains in my mind for a long time after. Anything he writes is a must-read."

Pink Quill Books

"Karl Drinkwater has the skill of making it near impossible to stop reading. Expect late nights. Simply outstanding."

Jera's Jamboree

"An intelligent and empathetic writer who has a clear understanding of the world around him and the truly horrific experiences life can bring. A literary gem."

Cooking The Books

"Drinkwater is a dab hand at creating an air of dread."

Altered Instinct

"A gifted writer. Each book brings its own uniqueness to the table, and a table Drinkwater sets is one I will visit every time."

Scintilla.info

TURNER

KARL DRINKWATER

ORGANIC APOCALYPSE

TURNER

Cover design by Karl Drinkwater

Published by Organic Apocalypse
ISBN 978-1-911278-01-6 (E-book)
ISBN 978-1-911278-00-9 (Paperback)
ISBN 978-1-911278-31-3 (Audiobook)

Organic Apocalypse Copyright Manifesto

Organic Apocalypse believes culture should be shared. We support far more reuse than copyright law and licensing organisations currently allow. We respect our buyers, reviewers, libraries and educators.

You can copy or quote up to 50% of our publications, for any non-commercial purpose, as long as the awesome source is acknowledged.

You may sell our print books when you've finished with them. Or pass them on to other people and share the love. You buy a copy, you own it.

We don't add DRM to our e-books. Feel free to convert between formats (including scanning, e-formats, braille, audio) and store a backup for your own use.

TURNER

Two Months Ago

Velocity. It was like flying three feet above the tarmac. Wind rushed against him, roared in his ears, and he let out a whoop of excitement. This was living: taking the turns in the road at high speed, every one a risk and a reward.

Rocketing down the next straight on his mountain bike, he tried to listen above the noise of the wind to hear if a car might be driving up to the hairpin bend ahead, hidden on the other side of the trees that separated lines of zigzagging road working their way down the steep hill.

He couldn't *hear* a car ... brake or not? Safety would dictate slowing down and staying in lane.

However, exhilaration dictated taking the bend at almost full speed, gambling that there *wasn't* a car coming the other way. He hadn't seen one for over half an hour. This really was an isolated stretch of coast.

The hairpin bend was just ahead now. The trees blurring past, a light-speed corridor of green, he didn't want it to end.

You only live once.

He tucked his elbows in and lowered his head, calculated the angle of the optimum racing line, gave the brakes the gentlest caress, drifted to the far right of the road into the oncoming traffic lane, and then threw all his weight to the left as the bike whooshed around the bend dangerously angled towards hard surface; stomach lurch when the tyres slipped a few inches on a patch of crunching loose gravel before biting back in, his room to manoeuvre reduced and the brown-green tree wall of the outer bend rushing scarily close; and then he was through, gradually drifting back into a long straight and sitting upright.

The imagined crash, ploughing into the front of an oncoming car, didn't happen, and Tom Stanley found he was grinning so widely it seemed like his face would split in two.

What a rush!

He felt so *alive.* He always did on these trips away from home on his beloved bike. Better than flying to one of the Balearic Islands for sex and drink and music; better than driving to France for cheese and duty free. This was exercise, and peace, and nature. The fortune he'd spent on the bike was worth it. And it *was* a fortune. Once while Tom was strapping his bike to the rack on his car he'd told a neighbour that the bike and kit had cost *more* than his (albeit second-hand) Toyota Avensis. The neighbour thought it was a joke.

It wasn't a joke.

Tom knew he could cover bigger distances with a touring bike rather than a mountain bike. Even when he locked out the suspension for hard pedalling sections his mountain bike was still nowhere near as efficient. But then he would miss out on the opportunity of going off-road when it presented: shortcuts downhill through woods, up banks, across streams, over rocks and logs. Thrills for the taking by those with the skill and strength to test themselves.

It was early afternoon and the green conifers whizzed past on either side, the sun flashing through their tips at the edges of his vision. This was one of the most wooded and isolated parts of Anglesey, and one of the few places in Wales he hadn't visited on his bike.

Tom needed these days by himself. Touring wasn't just a chance to get away from the pricks at work. It was also a release, an opportunity to stop being Tom Stanley for a while and be someone else. Or no-one. After each of these escapes he was full again, dynamo-charged, though he couldn't articulate what he had run out of.

Electricity, maybe.

Although it was a sunny day, the trees were so thick that there was deep shadow below them. Tom was keen to leave the woods and get back down towards the sea, to the last stretch of his journey. It would be good to rest; he had been cycling since eight o'clock that morning. Despite wearing the latest in lightweight Lycra – black cycling shorts and a yellow body-hugging top – he was still sweating copiously.

Then it was suddenly *all there*.

He realised that he wasn't hearing just the wind roaring in his ears as he sped along. It was the waves washing against the base of cliffs, one noise becoming another so subtly that it took him by surprise.

As the trees thinned out the road emerged onto a gorse-covered hill which fell away to the glittering sea, the only break for miles in the low cliffs. The shaded route he had come down swept up to Tom's right, making him feel vulnerably small.

He braked sharply to take in the amazing view, wheels crunching to a halt on loose stones. The sea was a carpet of white-flecked blue, too large to take in all at once.

He fumbled in his bum-bag for a map, opening it out across the handlebars while the sea breeze tugged at the corners.

If he read it correctly, he was closer than he'd thought. He had left Pen y Coed behind, and although the road followed the coast south for a while before running inland again, there would be a track somewhere before the headland; a track that would take him to his goal.

Eager to get going, Tom took a quick swig of water from his bottle, then put it back in its holder. He had food in his rucksack but would save that for later. For now he wanted to cover ground.

Flicking expertly through the gears, Tom was soon whizzing along past mixed gorse and grassland, occasionally seeing a few sheep in huge fenced-off sections of the hills.

He rode right past the turn-off at first, and had to cycle back, while a seagull shrieked its alien call overhead as if marking the spot. There was a grey dry-mud track running away from the road, with grass growing in the middle. It wasn't signposted, and was almost impossible to spot if you were heading south in the Beaumaris direction because it ran north then east, and was shielded by gorse bushes.

He had been warned that it wasn't easy to find, and nor was the place it led to – but that was the appeal for Tom. When Mike Betts had talked about it a few weeks ago, he had nicknamed it "the lost village". Not because it really was lost or abandoned, like some of the ones in Cornwall, Mike had explained drunkenly, but because that was how you felt when you got there. *If* you got there. Mike had wanted to talk about something else, but Tom wouldn't let it drop. He was forced to buy Mike more drinks before he would reveal the location, and what to look out for.

Tom freewheeled down the track a few metres, then got off the bike, propping it against a rowan covered in unripe berries. Getting his bearings, he strode over to a clump of bushes, and tugged some branches to the side. They hid an old and faded, algae-greened sign. It was almost as if nature were conspiring to hide the place.

The sign simply stated

Penrhyn

Peninsula

as Mike had said.

As he let the branches fall back into place, vaguely annoyed that no-one seemed bothered to tend the sign, he spotted something glinting further back from the road in a shadowed dip, thick with tangled plantlife.

Curious, he descended carefully down the loose scree, using a large grey boulder for support; his hand pulled a chunk of moss free as he nearly lost his footing. But he made it down and stepped over a thorny tangle of brambles, careful of his bare shins.

Broken glass in a shattered window. That was what had caught his attention. The car rested at an angle, the bonnet crumpled where it had come to a final halt against an outcrop of lichen-covered rock. The tyres were flat; rust attacked the frame, lifting off the red paint like scabs.

The weathered state of the small car suggested it had been there for some time. The number plates had been removed, leaving gaps like missing teeth. Tom glanced back up to the track he had left. There were no obviously damaged shrubs, ripped branches, bared earth or any other marks of a car's passing, so the car had left the road on this final short journey at least six months ago. Maybe a winter, maybe a year. Whatever. It had sat here ever since, while nature began the process of hiding the signs of this incursion. Abandoned by its owners to wait, alone, as it slowly crumbled into nothingness. It was somehow sad. A sense of abandonment came over Tom, the same as he felt when he was hill-walking and came across the tumbled, roofless walls of what must have been a sheep-farmer's cottage, but was now only an overgrown home to ghosts and ticks.

A gust from the sea rustled the shrubs around him. He peered in through the broken window. The upholstery was faded. There were a few dead leaves on the seats and dashboard. The glove compartment hung open. Tom noticed that the seatbelt on the passenger side dangled down and just ended. He reached in carefully, aware that the jagged glass edges might be old but they still looked sharp, and lifted the seatbelt. The end was frayed, as if it had been sawn through with a sharp edge unsuited for the job. The lower part of the seatbelt lay on the floor somewhere in shadow. It was cooler in the car.

Maybe the car had come off the road and the passenger seatbelt had jammed. The passenger might have been cut free.

With an unexpected shudder he dropped the seatbelt and scrambled back up to his bike, wiping his fingers absent-mindedly on his cycle shorts.

The track curved down and back, around a headland, and he finally got his first glimpse of Stawl Island. It surprised him, as if it had been lying in wait, a dark eye amongst the glittering, choppy waters.

It was about six miles long, north to south, and three and a half miles across at the widest point. The southern end was mountainous, with marshy lowland areas and dense woods near the middle. Towards the north the land rose again to become steep cliffs topped by a lighthouse standing proud against the elements. Apart from one spot where the land lowered to a sandbar, the coastline was either cliffs or jagged rocky shoreline. There was no harbour, and the island was obviously unsuitable for boats.

Connecting the island to the mainland was a sandbar nearly half a mile long, which reminded him of grey-yellow pus oozing from an infected sore. He had seen that kind of peninsula only once before: as a child his parents had taken him to the Isles of Scilly in Cornwall. A sandbar connected St. Agnes and Gugh, two of the islands. Happy memories of that time ignited for a few seconds, then snuffed.

The past is past for a reason.

Although the map Tom had looked at called it Stawl Island, he couldn't help wondering if it was technically an island, since it had a tentative connection to the mainland. Mike had told him it was only accessible like this sometimes; it was often cut off from the mainland completely, and not at times that were easy to predict (due to tides, currents, cliffs – "Shit like that," Mike had added authoritatively). That was another reason it seemed so lost – even when someone did see the dot of Stawl Island on a map of this sparsely-populated part of Anglesey and decided to visit, they might find it inaccessible. The bad signage, and the fact that due to quirks of geography it was only visible once you followed the track round the headland, were just the final nails in the coffin of Stawl Island.

Well, the sandbar was visible now, so Tom freewheeled down, seagulls gliding overhead. The sun shone, and out at sea the scudding clouds cast dark shadows, as if there were giant prehistoric plesiosaurs just below the surface.

The sandbar was surprisingly firm and easy to cycle over, suggesting a rock layer underneath. A few minutes of hard pedalling on the crunchy surface and he was across. He felt as excited as a first-dater as he cycled along the basic road which ran roughly east across the island, to the village he'd glimpsed from up on the mainland hills. A side road curved off to the south and disappeared beneath the canopy of thick oak woods, but he ignored that. After that the road ran through damp-looking low ground, which appeared desolate apart from the occasional scattered patches of oak. A sharp wind blew across this lowland, carrying the call of distant seabirds. Tom loved the fact that the only sounds here were natural ones, rather than traffic and music and noise that were ever-present back home. The road was so flat he was able to whizz along in a high gear, head tucked low, until finally the road forked into the two streets of the village.

The main road carried on straight, passing a shop, and old-fashioned shabby houses with grey-rendered walls, before the road ended at a chapel and graveyard. The side road skirted woods and passed a small mansion which overlooked the whole village. Tom remembered from the map that a track ran south from that building to an abandoned quarry in the mountain. However, the village was the end of the road.

It felt dead too. It just seemed so quiet.

Tom jumped off his bike at the junction and pushed it up the main street. On his right was a garage for repairing cars. A torn paper sign, which looked like it was from the 1950s, was pasted to the wall, saying "Griffiths Garage for SATISFACTION. Everything for the MOTORIST" in blue letters.

He nodded to a pair of older men sat on a bench in the forecourt. They just stared back. Tom felt theirs weren't the only eyes on him, but when he glanced at a house over the road the slight shift of yellowing lace in the partly-open window could easily have been a stirring in the breeze.

Tom accepted that he might be a novelty to these drably-dressed yokels. Here he was in shining Lycra, brightening up their rural lives. They probably didn't see many outsiders, especially ones with such good legs.

He looked back at the two men. One of them had got up and was striding down the side road as if on an urgent mission, head hunched forward and hands shoved into baggy jeans. He was soon out of sight around the corner. The other man wore a black hat with a round brim. He had a flattish, expressionless face, and was still staring at Tom. It unnerved him a bit, the man was so intense and ... unbothered by being overly rude. Maybe that was it.

"*Nedden,*" the man said.

"Sorry, are you talking to me?" Tom asked.

"*Arfilyn*," the man added, his deep black eyes glinting.

Tom walked on, puzzled, but still interested in his surroundings. His bike was so light he could easily guide it with one hand.

He was tutting mentally at the grubby state of some of the houses, that people let things decay so much, when from the alley between two buildings stepped a dark-haired girl whose striking looks made him stop in his tracks. Her hair was unkempt and wild, and her skin was so pale in contrast it looked like porcelain. She was about eighteen years old (nine years younger than Tom, but old enough), and would obviously be a stunning woman soon. She was wearing a long, plain skirt and faded beige blouse, clothes resembling hand-me-downs, but she was so attractive that the clothes seemed insignificant. It was hard to say what made her so beautiful – the contrasts of dark and light; beauty set off by drabness; the wildness in her eyes, which seemed to have more life than anything he had seen so far in the whole village.

He raised a hand and began to walk towards her, an unthinking, magnetic reflex. But when she saw him a strange expression crossed her face that made him drop his hand. It was almost like the shadow of a leer, and she darted back the way she had come, into the dark alley.

He looked around, wishing for at least one friendly face. There was a pub ahead. The name was in Welsh but the weathered sign included an image of a wrinkled and bearded old man snarling down at the road. It might not be the friendly face he wanted, but hopefully someone inside would be normal and could point him to a place to stay for the night. If not, he would be off and leave this dump behind. Tom had come in secret, so he could surprise Mike the next time he saw him by casually letting slip that he'd been here too – to the place that had spooked Mike. If he left straight away there wasn't much to boast about.

A man stepped out of the pub doorway, dressed in scruffy workman's trousers and a jumper with patched elbows. When his deep-set eyes passed over Tom, his frowning bushy eyebrows parted and he grinned.

Great: another yokel who has never seen a man in Lycra.

"*Sut hwyl gyfaill, ga i'ch helpu chi, y*?" the man asked.

"I'm sorry, I don't speak any Welsh." Tom had been in Wales for six years now, but had never got round to learning. Most people in Newtown spoke English anyway. He just knew enough to recognise the guttural *ch* sounds and the general accent as being definitely Welsh.

"Ah, that's no problem, I guess you're a tourist, then? Lost your way? Or just another friendly visitor to Pentref Bychan?"

"Is that the island's Welsh name?"

"*Diawl* no. It's this lovely village, my friend." He grinned still, as if he had made a joke. Maybe they knew irony here. Not a lost cause after all.

"Someone told me about this island, so I decided to visit. I love out-of-the-way places. I got the train as far as Holyhead, then cycled from there."

"Cycled, yeah?" The man looked at his bike.

"Well, yes. And I was thinking about staying here tonight, if there's anywhere I can get a room. It'd be fun to explore a bit before I get back, see what you've got here."

"Aye, see what we've got here." Still the inane grinning. The man scratched his scalp through thick, greying hair. "Tell you what. One of the houses in this road is empty. Used to be my Nain's, but she's gone now. Got her furniture in and everything. You could have that for a night if you wanted ..."

Suddenly he slammed a fist against the wall, making Tom jump. The man inhaled deeply and a strange wheezing sound came from his throat. Through the fit he still watched Tom out of the corner of his eye. Just as quickly it passed, and the man banged his palm against his chest.

"Ah, these lungs, play me up sometimes."

"Are you all right? Maybe you should see a doctor?"

"No doctors for me, I'm fine." He grinned again, his mouth stretched and plastic. "Yes, fine. Do you fancy the house for the night then? No-one needs it, so – you know – just for a bit o' cash. I guess yer on your own, so's there'd be lots of room."

"Yes, just me. It's very kind of you but –"

"No, not kind, a favour to both of us! I'll show yer in a minute if you like. Tell yer what, I'm just going to tidy it up. Why don't you go in the *tafarn* and have a drink? I'll come and get you in a bit. You'll need to know it anyway if you're staying here, isn't it? You'll have a thirst on you, I bet."

Tom didn't really want to take a full house, but couldn't think of a sane-sounding reason to refuse; besides, the man was so overtly friendly it would perhaps be mean to do so. "Well, okay."

"*Grêt!* Here, you go in here," the man pushed open the door to the pub, and Tom only just caught the name from him, which sounded like "Er Hen Theen". "Make yourself at home."

The man almost shoved him through the door, leaving Tom's bike propped against the wall outside.

As Tom's eyes adjusted to the darkness, he noticed that the few people inside were looking at him morosely. It didn't feel as welcoming as he had hoped.

"Erm, I can come with you if you want," Tom said to the man, "I don't even know your name."

"*Nage*, just stay here, have a nice drink. And Osian's my name." Then to the rest of the people in the bar, "*Mae'n saff, hogia, dydy'r Sais twp ddim yn dallt. Dw i am ddeud wrth yr arglwydd, os alla i.*" The man grinned at Tom, and the grin seemed somehow less than friendly. "You'll be fine mate, they'll look after yer. I'll be back soon, just wait. Enjoy." And he let the pub door swing shut with a bang, leaving Tom standing within, feeling more conspicuous in cycle shorts than he'd ever done before.

The pub only had small, dirty windows, so even after his eyes adjusted it was still gloomy. The decor was smoke-stained dark wood, and the notices (all in Welsh) were yellowed. There were a few men sat at tables, one at the bar, and a tall thin man behind the bar, in a grey shirt that was open to near the waist, as if he were proud of his narrow, hairless chest.

Tom walked over to him. "Hi," he said warmly, hoping to get a friendly response.

"Hi," the barman replied without any trace of warmth. "What do you want?"

Tom browsed the worn and scratched taps. "Carlsberg?"

"I think it's off. We don't do that kind of drink."

The barman grabbed a pint glass and held it under the tap that had a chipped Carlsberg logo above it. There was a bubbling squirt, like liquid shit, and something brown and cloudy spat into the glass, gobbing out in spurts until there were a few inches of murk in the bottom. He held it up. "Do you want it?" he asked, expressionless.

"No, thank you. I'll just have a gin and tonic."

"No tonic."

"Well, a whisky and coke then." He was trying not to lose his patience.

The barman took a tumbler and poured a shot of whisky, then opened a bottle of black coke with white marks where the glass had been scraped. He banged them on the bar in front of Tom. The whisky glass looked dirty but Tom kept that observation to himself and poured the coke in.

"How much do I owe you?" he asked.

"Settle up later."

Tom sipped the drink without enthusiasm, and tried to engage the barman in conversation about the island, but the monosyllabic answers soon stopped that.

Then the only other man sat at the bar shuffled his stool closer to Tom. He had ginger hair and a frayed baseball cap which with Shell embroidered across the front. He smelt of stale sweat. "Hello, you come here for the day, aye?"

"Yes, well, I might stay overnight."

"That's a good idea, yes, see the island's beauty – one of the jewels of the North, they say. Come on your own, then?"

"Yes."

The man shuffled his stool even closer, until he was practically leaning against Tom, intimidatingly strange and close. "Oh, you'll love us. We're friendly blokes here."

Love us seemed a strange choice of words.

"I haven't seen many women in the village. Only one girl in fact, who was she? Very pretty, black hair, pale face?"

The ginger man leaned closer, and the smell of sweat was overpowering. Tom had to make a conscious effort not to wrinkle his nose in disgust.

"Oh, Anne. She's lovely, a loving girl. We call her *Brân Ddu*."

"Brandy?"

"Near enough. She likes strangers. Sometimes."

"*Cau dy geg, Wil!*" snapped the barman suddenly and viciously, making Tom jump and the ginger man flinch. It seemed like a reprimand.

"No need for grumpiness in front of a guest now, is there?" Wil retorted.

The room brightened and Tom glanced round. Two more men came in, closing the door quietly. They stayed near the door, speaking in Welsh and occasionally glancing Tom's way. He felt like every eye was surreptitiously on him.

When he turned to his drink again the barman looked away, but for a fraction of a second it seemed as if he had been nodding at Tom, indicating something to the others in the bar. The fact that he looked momentarily guilty when Tom nearly caught him seemed to confirm that something was wrong. The atmosphere was pregnant with expectation. But for what?

Tom stood up. Immediately there was a subtle – but noticeable – edging closer of the people sitting or standing near the door; a readiness. On the surface they seemed nonchalant, but Tom felt as if they were blocking his exit.

Why?

He needed time to think, and didn't want to test his suspicion yet, in case it led to a confrontation. "Where are the toilets, please?" he asked his ginger-haired neighbour.

"Through those doors, then left," he said, pointing to the corner opposite the pub's entrance.

"Thanks."

On the other side of the door was a staircase going up, and a small room on his left with two more doors; the left one said *Merched* and the right, *Dynion*. Tom remembered the men's toilets in his favourite Newtown pub said *Dynion*, so pushed against that creaking door.

The toilets were as unpleasant as he'd expected. A smell of sour piss, and chipped tiles around the urinals. Tom moved quickly to the only toilet cubicle, locked the door, put the lid down, and sat on it.

What were the villagers planning? Or was he imagining it? His civilised self told him he was overreacting, but his instincts screamed that there was a threat here. But what? Would they mug him? Or something worse?

When he was younger, someone told him stories of an isolated moor where the army sent new recruits for survival training, and where the recruits sometimes disappeared, just leaving their pitched tents and equipment behind. No sign of them was ever found. In another version, the soldiers *were* found – but dead, with their throats cut, in a church. That apocryphal tale usually blamed Satanists, though neither version explained how a whole unit could be overpowered, except perhaps by a lot of people.

A lot of people in on something together.

As unlikely as the tales had seemed to him, the thought of them chilled him now.

Surely he couldn't be killed? To what end? People would find out, wouldn't they?

Then again, he had only mentioned to his mother where he was going this weekend. And if he disappeared, there would be no proof he ever actually *got* here – he had travelled a long distance. If everyone in the village denied seeing him, no investigation would get anywhere. The only likely outcome would be that his elderly mother would come herself to investigate ... which didn't bear thinking about.

He thought back to the rusting car, owners long gone after *something* happened.

Of course it was all stupid, he was a loony just for thinking of that. What would Mike say back in Newtown?

There was a noise outside the men's toilets. Whispers. Sounded like a few people. Tom froze. No-one came in, and the voices went quiet. He could feel himself panicking.

Climbing soundlessly up onto the toilet lid, he was able to examine the dirty window. It looked like it could be opened, but hadn't been for many years. Dead flies and moths lay on their backs all along the filth of the sill. The opening was small but a man might fit through.

The window was on the side of the pub, and Tom could see there was a wide gap between the pub and the next building – a garage with an old petrol pump in the forecourt.

He could also see a building further away – some kind of junkyard with a chain-link fence, off the smaller southern road of the village.

A few men dashed around there; the first people apart from Brandy to show any speed. Tom recognised the man who had said he could rent a house, apparently giving urgent instructions. He was reminded of a disturbed wasps' nest. A red pickup pulled out of the junkyard and halted by the men.

The driver jumped out – it was the man with ginger hair and the Shell baseball cap, Wil, who Tom had sat next to in the bar. Immediately he lifted something heavy out of the back of the pickup, helped by two men. It looked like a large, flat, stained piece of wood, with things dangling in the corners, possibly handles? Or straps? Someone else grabbed a toolbox, and they all moved out of sight towards the back of the pub, heaving the wooden thing with them.

Time must be running out, Tom thought. There were only two choices. Run or stay. If he ran and it turned out he was just being paranoid ... well, it was a minor embarrassment, which he would gladly suffer. If he ran and was right to do so, it could save his life. No contest.

He tried to open the window quietly, ignoring the dead insects. It seemed jammed.

Please don't be locked, please don't be locked.

In panic he used more force, hurting his hand in the process. He realised if he made a noise the people in the hallway might come in to investigate; as they might if he took too long.

The window finally moved, and he flushed the toilet, to give himself a few more seconds and hide the noise as the window was opened. He stuck his head out, and couldn't see anyone now. Perhaps they were at the back of the pub or inside it. The side of the building was in shade. Good – it could help to hide him. As the last of the flushing sounds died away he wormed his way out, bashing his hip bone badly. He tried to ignore the flash of pain and lower himself down.

He didn't fancy fleeing from the village on foot. He wouldn't get far before any pursuers caught up with him.

He was near the red pickup, but the engine wasn't running any more. The keys might be in the ignition, but to find out he would have to step into full view of anyone at the back of the pub. Besides, he hadn't driven anything other than an automatic for years and could see himself smacking into a building or getting stuck in the ditch trying to drive it back to the road. No, his bike was better.

He edged along the wall and peeped round the corner. There it was, still leaning against the front wall of the pub. The only person in view was an old man in a spotted shirt and patched trousers limping towards the pub, grey hair combed back. Now was his chance.

Not bothered if he looked silly to some back-country pensioner, Tom crouched and hurried past, below the pub windows. The bike was right next to the main door. Heart pounding, he grabbed it, faced it out of the village and jumped on. He felt better once he began to move.

The old man smiled, creating more cracks in his dry, weather-beaten face, and beckoned to Tom, walking straight in front of the bike. Tom swerved but didn't stop. "Iwan! Iwan!" the old man shouted.

Other people appeared from houses now, and, glancing back, he saw three men dashing out of the pub. A car door slammed and an engine revved into life. The pickup.

If he cycled out of the village and headed across the sandbar, he'd be caught in two minutes. He wouldn't even make it as far as the turn-off for the woods.

Someone appeared out of nowhere, and nearly knocked him off his bike. People were rushing over, yelling to each other in Welsh.

The plan had to change.

He swerved left at almost full speed and took the small lane that led to the old quarry. He might be able to lose the truck on that, and could certainly outrun anyone following on foot. Hopefully he could then head off-road past the woods and back to the sandbar. If he cycled like hell, and used every ounce of ability he'd built up over the years, he might do it before they realised his intentions.

Tom was going so fast he almost didn't see a bald, fat man step out of the school grounds. Tom leaned the bike left and avoided him, but whizzed into the junkyard, slamming on the brakes just before he hit a rusty tractor-trailer, the bike's back wheel skidding until he faced the gate he'd come through.

The fat man stood at the junkyard gate, and already others were running up.

Tom scanned the yard; there was a corrugated iron shack in one corner, and the rest was scrap metal, piles of tyres, and the rusting skeletons of lots of plateless cars – a surprising amount for such a small settlement. The whole yard was surrounded by a chain-link fence twelve feet high.

Shit.

The small group at the gate made way for the red pickup, which crunched to a stop on loose gravel, the door opening immediately. The ginger-haired man leapt out, fingering his baseball cap agitatedly but smiling. "Hey, what are you running for, *bach*?" He walked forward slowly, but Tom saw the gate being closed behind him. As it clunked into place two men stayed by it, while others advanced slowly behind Ginger. "There's nothing to worry about," he said. "We aren't going to hurt you."

"Why are you chasing me then?" Tom yelled, and realised he was crying with fear.

"To get the money for your drink. You didn't pay!"

Tom wanted to believe him. He wanted to so much.

Ginger slipped a hand into a pocket, and kept it there. As if he was holding something. "Just going to talk."

Tom cycled away from the gate. The men ran after him. He reached the pile of tyres, shouldered his bike and scrambled up. It was hard to keep his footing, but he didn't dare ditch the bike.

Come on you bastard! he urged himself silently. *You've run with the bike before, so you can fucking climb!*

The men were gaining as he got to the rubber peak, within three feet of the top of the chain-link. He threw the bike over and it crashed to the ground on the other side, wheels first, bounced once at an angle then clattered prone – he was glad he hadn't fully locked out the suspension. Then he clambered up and over, dangling by his hands before dropping the last five feet or so, just as the men reached the top of the tyre pile.

"*Cachwr!*" someone yelled.

Tom jumped on the bike and started back along the lane to the quarry track. The bicycle seemed undamaged. He risked a rearwards glance. Most of the men were scrambling back down the tyre pile towards the pickup truck and junkyard gate – he'd definitely bought some time there. The two who dropped over the fence after him would soon be left behind, though they were running as best they could.

There were yells coming from many directions now.

Tom cycled past the last building on the right – the small mansion he'd seen earlier. It had a walled garden, and as Tom passed he thought he glimpsed someone watching him from a window above the Doric columns of the porch.

It didn't matter; only the cycling mattered, getting in the rhythm, heart pumping in time with his legs, breathing in time with the revolutions of the wheels, every ounce of speed coming from the controlled rhythms of man and machine in harmony.

He went up a track away from the village. He was a good way along, passing woods on his right, when he heard the engine revving behind him. The truck was gaining, though thankfully not too fast – the roughness of the disused trail saw to that. Still, he probably wouldn't make the quarry before the truck caught up.

Plan B (as if there was ever an A).

The grass by the track here wasn't too long to cycle over. He veered off the path on the right side and headed west. Instead of leaving the woods behind and carrying on, he could skirt them. It would take him back to the road, some distance from the village. The truck would either have to try and follow over even rougher country, or go back the way it had come and try to head him off.

Even better, they might assume he would hide in the woods, amongst the thick cover of bracken, bramble, oak and heather, and waste time looking for him there.

He was far from safe, but dared to hope.

His heart was racing as fast as the bike, and he allowed himself to doubt, just for a few seconds. What if it really was just a quiet village full of inbred bumpkins? What if they always went quiet when a stranger entered the pub? The men by the door in the pub could have been waiting for friends; the people whispering outside the toilet could have been secret lovers or having a private chat. Tom's mind seized on this, because it removed some of the fear, at least temporarily.

The coughing house-owner could have been looking for help to prepare the house; the old man could have been calling a friend's name. Hell, he *had* snuck out of the pub without paying after acting strangely, and apparently running away after arranging to rent a house – it wasn't surprising their friends went after him for money or an explanation.

It wasn't surprising their friends helped out, and the more he ran the more annoyed they got. He could have just read too much into –

Blinding pain shot through him, and for seconds he couldn't move. He realised he was lying on his back staring up at a gloriously blue sky, floating like the clouds but with the pain; something was trickling into his ear, and a wheel was spinning nearby, whirring, whirring, round and round and round.

It stopped.

He lifted his head slightly, blinking hot sticky fluid from an eye. One of his arms wouldn't move, it was twisted behind him somehow. Funny, he didn't mind too much, if only he could focus his eyes properly, and if only the pain in his head would go. Once he made the spinning noise start again he could look at the clouds and float and float.

He squinted and blinked. It was his bike. With one foot on the wheel and his back to Tom was a large man in a bright red plastic raincoat with the hood up.

That was why the nice spinning had stopped. But why wasn't he on his bike still?

The man walked towards Tom with a limp, and something dangled from his right arm.

A big piece of wood.

The man pulled his hood down but Tom still couldn't see his face clearly, because of that nasty sticky stuff in his eye, but it seemed somehow wrong, more than just blurred.

"I want to fly again," Tom said, head falling back.

The clouds.

"I want to float."

The strange man was standing over him now, a smudge of red like a big balloon.

"You can float," said Tom dreamily as the man lifted his right arm.

"Run, you idiots!"

The small and smartly-dressed man strode through the woods, yelling at the villagers to move more quickly. He swung his crop hard at a middle-aged man as he scurried past, speeding him on his way with a stinging blow to the shoulder.

His excitement made him feel young, but he was concerned.

This was an impromptu taking: unusual, but viable when the circumstances were favourable. If an apple falls into your hand you would be a fool to throw it away. So when the breathless messenger had turned up at his home and given him the details it only took a moment's thought before he authorised the chase. *Carpe diem*, and all of that.

Branches cracked as some of the men ahead of him tore through the brush, no doubt fighting tiredness as much as the tangles of this obstacle-filled wood. His own greying hair was combed with a gentleman's cream and had a parting from the left temple backwards, but was thrown into disarray by an over-hanging limb. He smoothed it back with his hand.

The screaming reached his ears from the far side of the Coed Gwalltog woods, and he sighed. That was a cause for concern. The woods-haunting Bwystfil was obsessed with cutting things up. He should never have made a hunter its mentor, such a shame.

He hoped the villagers got there before it was too late to salvage anything. There were better uses for the man.

The Logging Camp

> "Good luck comes in slender currents, misfortune in rolling tides." – Irish proverb

"Motherfucker!" Chris cursed the red-thorned brambles that had scratched his arm. Miniscule droplets of blood welled into lines. He wiped a hand over the scratches, and saw the lines redraw themselves.

He should have walked along the road from the village, *then* turned off and followed the track to the logging camp. Instead he'd tried to make up time by taking this short cut through the Coed Gwalltog. He now saw why no footpaths crept through this wood. The oak and wild cherry at the edge, which had looked so passable, had quickly given way to bramble run riot and treacherous ground hidden by bracken.

It was just his luck. Nothing went right for him. If it did he would be sunning himself somewhere hot and dry right now, with a bimbo at his side, not lying low on this shithole Welsh island looking for work.

"You shouldn't go through the woods."

Chris turned, surprised at the heavily Welsh-accented voice. Stood by a holly tree, feet firmly planted and arms folded, dressed in a spinsterish long grey skirt, white top and black cardigan, was the strange girl from the village.

Most of the village women were rarely seen, except during services in their chapel. Chris assumed the society here was ultra-conservative, where kids knew their place and where women mostly stayed indoors.

Apart from this girl, Anne Jenkyns, who always seemed to be around.

Chris didn't like her. She *was* beautiful, he'd admit. But there was something strange about her. Maybe she was a bit simple or had some mental problem. He couldn't really explain it, but the few times he'd spoken to her, the word that occurred to him most frequently was *trouble*. It was the way she looked at him; if he caught her gaze, it seemed sexual and hungry. In this kind of village, giving in to those kinds of girls was never a good idea, even if he hadn't felt an unaccountable repulsion towards her.

Lie low, keep out of trouble and he would be okay. Making moves on a weird, lusting farmer's daughter on a remote island would have been breaking the rules.

He stared at her impatiently.

"There's the *Bwgan Bach Llanfychan. Siarad Cymraeg, dach chi*?"

"No, I don't."

"Shame." She eyed him up disconcertingly. "It refers to the red goblin. It haunts the island's woods, they say. We don't normally mention it to outsiders, but I am willing to warn *you*."

"I've never been scared of goblins or legends," said Chris, as he turned and started walking away from her.

"Oh, you should be." Instead of taking the hint she trotted up behind him, and walked to his left.

"Go away," he said.

"It's more my island than yours, I'll go where I want. I like the tattoo on your hand. Is it a seagull?"

She reached out, took his wrist, and raised his left hand to her eyes to examine the tattoo more closely. He snatched his hand back.

"You don't smile," she said, unperturbed.

"Nor do you."

"Do you believe in God?"

Despite himself, he laughed. "I shouldn't admit it to someone who spends so much time in chapel, but no. Never been any evidence that I could see."

"What about demons?"

"Oh hell, yes. I've seen plenty of those."

He pushed through a line of bushes and finally broke free of Coed Gwalltog. Heathland beyond. As they crossed it a few scraggy sheep were surprised by their appearance and bounded off amongst the green and brown bracken and spiky gorse clumps

"Where are you going?" she asked, still following.

"I'm hoping to get a job."

He'd not had much luck on the work front since arriving. The quarry he'd noted on the map was disused; the islanders didn't go out fishing because the cliffs and currents made the island unsuitable for boats, and any other fishing was done from the low points of the broken, rocky coast of the island by individuals with their own tackle. No employment there. The few odd jobs he'd got had only just been enough to make it worth staying. Until now he'd been refused work at the logging camp, though Iwan (the skinny, morose bastard barman, landlord of the pub he was staying at, the Hen Ddyn) said that some of the itinerants at the camp had done a runner and Iwan had heard there was a place now for a man of Chris's qualifications.

By which Chris assumed Iwan was thinking strong, silent, and apparently stupid.

"With the loggers?"

"Yes."

Ahead was the wood called Hen Goed. He could skirt it to the north until he reached the road to the logging camp. After that the woods were almost impenetrable, apart from where the loggers had done their work.

Fat blobs of rain pattered down from the slate-grey sky. No luck with the weather either.

He just hoped he would have luck getting a job. Iwan had told him to be at the logging camp for 11am, and that had been Chris's intention. But half a bottle of whisky last night had put paid to that idea. So now he was hours late for seeing the gaffer. He hoped it would be okay. They worked all day, didn't they? It wasn't a bloody office job. But his head was still banging, which didn't help his mood.

Maybe – just maybe – his bad luck was at least partly his own fault, he mused.

"It isn't nice to cut down trees."

"Could be I'm not a nice bloke. And if so you'd best be running home."

"I'm not scared of any *man*," she said.

"You obviously haven't met some of the men I know."

"Oh yes? And how do you know bad men?"

"I wish you would shut up."

"So now you don't want me to go away?"

"I want that too, but I don't think you will."

Despite his increased pace and longer legs he couldn't leave her behind. She seemed able to step around obstacles, never catching her clothes; whereas every bramble seemed to snag on his jeans, and every hole hidden by grass seemed to want to trip him up.

They reached the Hen Goed and followed its edge. He stayed under the shelter of the outer trees where possible, in the vain hope of staying drier. She didn't bother, and her black hair was soon plastered down in wet strands. Yet she seemed to exult in the wind and rain.

Loony.

Sometimes he hated being here. The surly, ill-looking villagers. The permanent dampness and bad weather. The lack of comforts. It had only been two weeks, but he missed strolling through a busy city centre on a Saturday night, crowd-watching.

He had to admit it had its pluses though.

There was no big police force looking for him.

No temptations to break the law.

Hell, hardly any outsiders either – the craze for Welsh holiday homes seemed to have passed this island by.

A place at the edge of nowhere, with a history of drifters who stay a bit then disappear again, an ideal place for someone who just wants work with no questions.

That's the advantage of such surly villagers. No questions (present company excepted). The locals barely even *spoke* to him. Bonus. Apart from the poncey little Lord who wanted to know all sorts of things. It wouldn't surprise him if the so-called Lord wanted to know how many times his "subjects" shat in a day, as well as the colour and size of their turds.

Still, he hadn't seen him for a few days, so that was good too.

The girl stopped suddenly, head cocked. "The chapel bell."

"Well whoopee doo." He could barely hear it.

"You will get your wish now. I need to return to the village. But maybe I can walk with you another time?"

Chris just grunted and walked on.

"You are interesting," she called after him before turning to make her way back.

Chris wasn't into religion. He didn't even know the name of the chapel, and had certainly never set foot inside it. That was just something for the villagers, a religious lot, judging by the number of times they went to services.

He soon reached the access to Hen Goed. The track ran into the depths, and the rough-barked old trees pressed in from both sides, hungry to reclaim the land. Most of the leaden sky was hidden from view within ten feet by the huge canopies of ancient oaks. It seemed much quieter here; the noise of the sea was blocked by the gnarled, massive trunks, replaced by the similar but more subdued rustle of leathery leaves.

The rain became heavier, and dripped through from above. Chris wished he had got here for eleven. Then he'd have been back at the pub before the rain hit. He had a feeling this could be quite a storm.

He walked faster and soon came to the logging camp. It was in a large clearing. Presumably they had started inside the wood, rather than at the edge, so the few tourists who came to Stawl Island wouldn't see what a mess the loggers were making.

The ground was all churned earth, branches, and mammoth tree stumps thrusting out of the ground like the stumps of an amputee. Which they were, in a way. Chris felt a pang of guilt that he would be helping them destroy all these trees; trees that were old when he was a baby. He was no nature-lover, preferring the joys of the big city, but this still seemed like a desecration.

It would only be for a while, he told himself.

The actual camp consisted of a large portable cabin, a shack that was probably an equipment storage shed, and various vehicles: truck trailers (some empty, some with logs on), industrial harvesters, shredders, and a bulldozer. Between all those were felled trees and huge piles of wood chips.

Rain assaulted Chris again as he left the protection of the foliage. The clearing was dark, the sky now deep grey. He skirted round the first pile of logs and the bulldozer before he realised what was bothering him – there was no-one around. No noise of machinery or chainsaws either.

Maybe it was a tea break.

"Hello?" Chris called, "Anyone here?"

Only the pattering of rain, darkening the dry chips of wood on the ground. Nearby was a yellow safety helmet abandoned in the churned-up mud.

He headed over to the portable cabin that must serve as the office. On the way he glanced into the cab of one of the vehicles – the keys were in the ignition. There must be *someone* around; the equipment wouldn't be left unguarded for thieves to take or vandals to wreck.

Then again, this wasn't city life any more.

The portable cabin was about forty feet long, and raised off the ground on steel legs. Chris knocked on the door and it rattled – it was just pulled to, not locked. Chris thought he heard a voice, or a noise (a chair moving?), then there was silence. He expected someone to open the door or shout "Come in", but no-one did.

He pulled the door open and climbed the aluminium steps, into the shack and out of the rain. The only window was over the sink to his left, letting in a pale half-light. There was a fridge-freezer, a small gas stove, some electrical equipment on the side and a pile of paperwork. To the right was a door to the next room, and some kind of large storage cupboard.

"Hello? I've come about a job."

Still the silence.

"Look, is there anybody here? I'm not into hide-and-seek."

Chris moved over to a folding table and picked up a newspaper, which was open at a photo of some topless eighteen-year old. He strained to read the cover in the gloom – yesterday's copy. He dropped it back on the table where it landed in a puddle of tea. There were three cups there – one empty, one half-full and one on its side. The last one mustn't have been empty when it was tipped over.

Rain spat against the panes of glass with a crackling noise just as the door banged, making Chris spin round.

No-one.

Only the wind.

He closed the door until the catch clicked this time, then moved over to the large store cupboard. Inside were jackets and hard hats, and a shelf at the top was home to a long Maglite torch and first aid kit. On the floor chains were piled against cardboard boxes, which in turn pushed against assorted tools leaning in the corner.

As he closed the cupboard door he heard a noise in the next room. He froze. Like a guttural croaking, and a cough, but with hints of words, which stopped as abruptly as it started.

Someone was in there.

Chris reached into the cupboard. Amongst the tools was a three-foot long, smooth axe handle. He took it out, hefted it, liking the balance. Then he used the tip of it to push open the door to the next room.

The blinds were three-quarters down, so it was even darker. He could see vague outlines of cabinets and furniture as his eyes adjusted. Nothing moved.

"Hello?" he said once more, not expecting a reply, and not getting one.

He edged along the outer wall, axe handle loosely held down at his side in his left hand; the hand with the tattoo of a seagull on the back, a remnant from his only stint in prison. He was almost at the window when the noise came again from a desk nearby.

He yelled “Shit!” and raised the handle to strike, while his right hand yanked the blinds to the side so he could see better.

Then he laughed.

On the desk was a CB radio set, crackling and popping with interference. Someone had left the bastard on. He was glad no-one had seen him getting so tense over something so daft.

Pulling the blind up and fastening it, he saw that this was the office. A few desks and tables, filing cabinets, and the radio set.

The garbled message came through again – amongst the hissing he just made out a few words, which sounded Welsh, possibly shouting, but too crackly to understand even if he knew the language.

He fumbled around for a power switch, and the set whined into silence.

He hated gadgets like that: radios, computers, mobile phones. Electrical shit. He didn’t understand them and didn’t want to.

He jumped down to the ground outside the shack, landing with a squelch in a thick layer of mud. The rain was heavier, and he didn’t want to hang around long. The place gave him the creeps.

Something flapping on the door of the bulldozer cab caught his eye. He squelched over. A yellow workman’s jacket, half in, half out. He eased the door open and unhooked the coat. The zip was broken. Maybe the sleeve got caught on a handle inside. But why leave it like that?

He bundled it onto the seat and closed the door, then walked cautiously back to the track out of the wood. There was still no sign of anyone. Once he got to the track he tossed the axe handle into the undergrowth, pulled up the collar of his polo shirt and trudged back to the village. Thunder rumbled overhead.

The rabbit was still alive but weak; the snare had wrapped around its throat but not completely strangled it as it struggled at the base of a solitary, crinkly-leaved alder.

Meurig Evans knelt by it, put on thick gloves in case it had enough strength left to scratch, and removed it from the snare.

Then he snapped its neck with a well-practised twist, and put it in the sack. This one would do.

He knew the routes through the oak and downy birch trees so well that he paid no attention to where he put his feet amongst the heather. He hummed tunelessly to himself, gripping the sack tightly in one hand.

Back at the decrepit hunting lodge he admired his own handiwork – the animal skins stretched tight across the door, so that none of the original wood could be seen. He liked that, running his (now gloveless) hand over the surface, feeling the different textures of the various skins; the different sensations if you went with or against the fur; the thread roughly stitching the skins together. Rabbit, fox, deer, otter, some white seal-calf.

He went into the lodge. Remains in here too as a variety of animal skulls hung on the wall. Also some leghold traps he liked to use, including the biggest, for *special* quarry; particularly large or dangerous things. He bolted the door behind himself, and closed the fraying curtains.

A large thick rug of stitched sheepskins lay on the wooden floor in the centre of the room. He pulled it back, revealing a trapdoor. Padlocked. He unlocked it with the keys on his belt, and lifted it until at a certain angle the chain caught and it stayed open. He descended the wooden steps, which creaked under his weight. Light came down here and pooled at the bottom, but no further. The room was shadow.

"*Paid â ffugio cysgu. Rwyt ti'n edrych arna i, dw i'n gwybod.*" ["Don't pretend to be sleeping. You're watching me, I know."]

A grunt from the dark.

Meurig threw the dead rabbit to the edge of the light; large hands snatched out of the darkness, grabbed it, and disappeared again. There was a low groan, then wet tearing and slurping noises.

"*Diwrnod lwcus. Ti'n cael mynd allan heddiw, Bwystfil. Mae'n bryd.*" ["Lucky day. You're allowed out today, Beast. It's time."]

The Woods

"Roar through the woods, and make whole forests fall." – Homer, *The Iliad*

David Smithwick wore an unbranded blue tracksuit with a white stripe down each side, and was running as fast as he could. His legs ached. He leapt over a dip in the ground and risked a glance behind. His pursuer was gaining.

He redoubled his efforts but knew he wouldn't last much longer. He could sense the hot breath at his heels, and in one last effort tried to run round a clump of gorse, but it was no good. His pursuer leapt at him, spinning him and knocking him onto his back, and he lay there with the drooling snout just a few inches from his face.

"Spotty, you daft dog!"

Spotty kept licking his face in excitement, until – still laughing – David pushed him off and stood, brushing damp and dead bracken from his tracksuit bottoms.

Spotty sat wagging his tail and watching David.

"You're not meant to knock me over! What if I'd landed on some gorse or a thistle? You wouldn't get any treats when we got back then, would you, eh?"

Spotty rolled on his side with his legs open.

"Put it away!" laughed David.

He walked away and Spotty followed.

This island was great for running. A world away from Swansea, where he had last been posted. He'd enjoyed it there for a while, but when a fellow officer had been stabbed while trying to calm two men arguing outside a club it was the last of many straws. He'd undergone a post-trauma psychiatric evaluation, and been recommended for a career break. However, he hadn't wanted that – he'd just wanted to go somewhere different, somewhere that reminded him of his childhood in Herefordshire, near the English border with Wales, somewhere like the world they'd portrayed in *Heartbeat* on TV.

He could still scarcely believe that he'd found it.

When he had heard through the police grapevine about the island, with one police officer, who was about to retire, leaving a vacant post in the South Anglesey District Moelfre Ward, David applied immediately. He had to be interviewed of course, but to everyone's surprise the city officer fitted the bill.

Welsh language? Check. Thanks to six years' of adult education classes, followed by a short intensive course before applying for the transfer.

Experience? Check. Signed up for police training nine years ago at the age of eighteen in Shrewsbury; in Swansea for the last six.

Suited to a remote rural environment? Check. Brought up in one, and yearning to get back; hobbies include running and trying to train a wayward Labrador.

Could cope with somewhere in which there was virtually no recorded crime, which could get boring? Check. It was exactly what the doctor ordered – well, police psychiatrist.

So here he was, newly moved into a house near the police station in the village of Pentref Bychan. It was the only real settlement on Stawl Island – the bastardised English form of its Welsh name, *Ynys Diawl*. Devil Island.

When he had looked into it before coming, David was pleased to find nothing too ominous or strange in the history books. True, it had been a base for piracy and skulduggery, mainly in the thirteenth century, and that was apparently where the name Ynys Diawl came from. Not because of the rumours of Satanic masses as he had read in one old book – that was just a story that came about later, probably based on a misunderstanding about the name of the island. The island inhabitants spent so much of their time in the chapel, Capel yr Arglwydd (The Lord's Chapel), that Satan wouldn't be able to come within ten miles of Ynys Diawl.

He could see where visitors' negative views of the island came from, though. With the exception of Lord John ap Ynyr Fychan most of the other native residents were hard work: insular, quiet, and wary of strangers. Nonetheless David was hopeful they would take to him, given time.

Yes, they were surly, but the island was a safe, crime-free place. As the current Lord explained when David first arrived, islanders didn't lock their doors. The Lord said it was liberating to leave your door unlocked and still sleep safe in the knowledge that no harm could come. He had encouraged David to follow their custom, smiling up at him with a piercing stare. It sounded nice, but old habits die hard, and Swansea hadn't worn off yet.

Anyway, until he was accepted he had Spotty for company. And there was his current mentor, Police Constable Emyr Huws, who had been born on the island, lived here all his life, was now being forced to retire (one of the few subjects he would morosely talk about until the tide came in), and would no doubt eventually die here. Though "mentor" might not be the correct word for someone who spoke to David little more than the other villagers did. David knew that Emyr wasn't happy with his successor. Still, David could bide his time, pick up the few ropes, and when Emyr retired things should improve. He tried to be optimistic about that.

For now exploring the island on long, energetic runs with Spotty was the perfect antidote to the sometimes-tense atmosphere in Pentref Bychan. Every cloud has a silver lining, David's mum used to say. Possibly even the grey ones gathering overhead.

And there were so many places he loved to run. For a half-hour energiser there was the route around Coed Gwalltog south-west of the village (the "hairy wood", so named because of the dense brambles; it was easier skirted around than gone through). For a longer endurance test there was the path to the old quarry on Mynydd Mawr at the southern end of the island, which was close to a beautiful stream that ran down the mountain and off the eastern side, falling to the sea in a fantastic waterfall which held all the colours of the rainbow on a sunny day. Another favourite was to take Spotty to the sandbar, and they would run along it when the tide was out – David barefoot, to feel the coarse sand crunch between his toes.

The only place he avoided was inside the oak scrub wood in the middle of the island, Coed Derwen. There was a hunting lodge there, and the hunter, Meurig Evans, who supplied trapped and hunted meat to the village, was even more morose and strange than the villagers. As you got near the lodge you'd find dead animals grotesquely nailed to trees. David had seen rabbits, birds, even a slow-worm. He preferred to stay away.

Today he'd taken the track north-west of the village. The rain fell more heavily so David ran towards Glanmor Fach woods where he might remain drier until the storm passed over. Spotty loped along beside him, excited by the sense of urgency.

They soon reached the woods and slowed to a strolling pace as they followed the path. The trees broke up some of the rain, which sounded calming as it drummed on the leafy roof above. They were mostly native oak, as all the woods on the island were, but a few grey-barked beeches grew here and there. The green, angled twigs of bilberries were common here too, and as he approached the edge of a clearing he realised he was near a patch rich with fat, dark purple fruits. David couldn't resist sampling them and enjoying another of the benefits of the island's wildness, so he carefully selected those which were ripe, dropping the over-soft spoiled ones on the ground. The berries were sweet, moreish, and before he knew it his fingertips were stained red. In the greyness they looked unnervingly like bloodstains. He stared at his fingers for a long while, thoughtful. He didn't eat any more berries after that.

He was preparing to dash across the clearing to the cover of the other side, where the path continued, when he heard a low growl from Spotty.

It wasn't like him to snarl. He was such a soft-natured dog that David secretly worried that Spotty would be more of a hindrance than a help in an arrest situation (though the image of Spotty licking a criminal's face until he submitted gave him a wry smile).

"What is it, boy?"

He rested his hand on Spotty's head, and noticed the dog's hackles were raised, head lowered. He was *really* unhappy.

"It's okay, boy – there are no bears on the island." His eyes scanned the direction in which the dog was staring: the side of the clearing away from the path. All he could see were trees and shadows.

"Come on, Spotty, you're starting to spook me."

It was true. There was a stillness in the air, an expectancy that the birds seemed to sense as well. They were all silent.

A throaty rumble of thunder overhead startled David, and suddenly Spotty was off, dashing across the clearing and into the copse opposite, barking. David ran a few steps but it was too late to grab his collar; he yelled for Spotty to come back, but he was ignored. He cursed.

Spotty ran out of earshot, and it was quiet again. The woods were as secretive and dark as before, but more menacing now that they had swallowed up the dog.

He knew he should follow; leave the path and wander through the forest until he found Spotty and clipped his lead back on. The dog had just been spooked by the thunder, that's all. He was probably chasing a squirrel.

But in his throat David could feel the same dryness he felt when Constable Clavin had been stabbed in front of him. His palms sweated, yet his eyes – still locked on the trees – were dry. He walked briskly, scanning every shadow. The path came out on the other side of the wood, where Spotty was bound to be.

After a while he even plucked up the courage to call out the dog's name.

The woman nervously placed the bowl of *cawl* in front of the man. She wore an old-fashioned thick black dress with a large collar, the lack of any brightness continuing upwards to her curly hair and dense eyebrows.

Her husband hadn't cleaned up yet, and his dark jacket smelt of fish. He still wore his high cap with a small peak at the front. He looked at the bowl, thick beard only a few inches above the surface of the soup. Bits of unidentifiable gristly meat sat in the grey liquid with the vegetables; small rafts of congealed fat floated on top.

"*Dw i ddim yn siwr am hyn, Peredur; dw i 'di bod yn poeni, dw i 'di bod yn cael hunllefa' bob nos. A ti; ti 'di bod yn sgrechian yn dy gwsg, dydy o ddim yn naturiol. A dy iechyd, dydy o ddim cystal rŵan. Mae'n oer allan, yn gynnar, ond est ti allan a –*" ["I'm not sure about it, Peredur. I've been worrying, I've been having nightmares every night. You too; you've been calling out in your sleep, it isn't natural. And your health, it isn't so good now. Cold out there, early, but you still went out and –"]

Without even looking he swung his bony fist back, connecting with her chin. Her head snapped sideways and she stumbled into the dresser, knocking over the picture of Peredur holding a six pound bass. It fell to the floor and the glass smashed.

"*Dyna araith hir iawn fanna rŵan. Ond aros di mewn, os nad wyt ti isho bod yn rhan o betha, ddynas,*" he mumbled. ["There was a great long speech, now. But just stay in, if you don't want to be involved, woman."]

She put her hand to the throbbing pain in her chin – it came away red. A split lip. She removed the spotted scarf that had been tied around her neck and held it against her lips. Something burnt in her eyes and she ran up the stairs.

Peredur ate the soup, staring blankly ahead.

The small man stood near the top of Mynydd Mawr at the south end of the island, so as to gain the best view across the land. The canopy of a graceful ash tree protected him from the rain, though the wind whipped his oiled greying hair from its neatly-combed perfection. Every now and again he smoothed it back with his palm.

The road from the mainland ran in from the west side, splitting so that a southern branch ran into the logging camp of the Hen Goed, whose ancient oak woods grew up to the base of Mynydd Mawr; and the other branch ran east to Pentref Bychan, where the man's mansion was. The village also contained the ancient stone chapel, which had originally been founded during the Age of the Saints – from here he could just make out the large sculptured wheel-head stone cross next to it, nine feet high, like an arthritic bony finger pointing upwards out of the earth.

The island reminded him of a heart. A healthy heart.

He rarely enjoyed the silliness of metaphors but decided to indulge himself.

Firstly, the island sat in a sea of liquid, protected.

Secondly, the road was an artery, bringing fresh life to the island; and a vein, taking blood out for renewal and exchange, removing things, such as trees from the wood.

No. That didn't work. Arteries *left* hearts, and veins brought blood back for oxygenating. How foolish of him – a scientist – to mix that up. That is what happens when one gives in to fancy.

He sighed, his shoulders slumped.

The road did act like a dividing line though.

Above it the marsh, then Coed Derwen, spread across the island. He could see the delicate traceries of tracks which stretched out to the beach and sea caves in the north-east, and the lighthouse to the north. It stood out because of the white walls around the base, acting as a navigation aid, even in the daytime when the light wasn't on. His gaze continued north-west to Glanmor Fach, with its cliffside picnic area so beloved of tourists.

Below the road was Coed Gwalltog, near the village, so thick with brambles and holly as to be almost impenetrable, and Hen Goed to its south-west. He followed the lie of the land as it rose to Mynydd Mawr, this throne of rock. To his right was the disused stone quarry and mine, with the Twll Twrw cave descending into the blackness beneath the earth. Beyond that the stream that weaved down the mountain before cascading off Allt-Wen cliff.

From the sandbar to the deep sea caves, it was all his domain. *All.* And today everyone would know that fact, and tremble.

The Happy Camper

> "Am I in earth, in heaven, or in hell? Sleeping or waking, mad or well-advised?" – Shakespeare, *The Comedy of Errors*

The sea was becoming choppy, white spume speckled the surface where the waves fought, while the masochistic crashing of breakers against the base of the cliffs echoed upwards and reached her as a dull roar.

The sky was grey right down to the horizon, and in a few places the horizon was no longer visible – obscured by the huge walls of advancing rain suspended between almost-black clouds at the top, and the huge grey shadow over the sea below.

Megan shivered, wrapped her blanket tighter around her shoulders and took another sip of weak tea from her chipped enamel cup. The wind was picking up too on this exposed spot at the edge of the cliffs on the north-east end of the island, just above a cove and south of the lighthouse.

She would pack her tent and camping stove up once she had finished her tea and veggie bacon sandwich. Then perhaps spend another half-hour in the bird-watching hut at the edge of the cliff (even if it did smell a bit of urine, and had graffiti inside it), before deciding where to go next.

This place was so beautifully bleak. Even the wild wind and rain filled her with wonder at the forces of nature. So she didn't mind that the radio had forecast a huge storm. She could retreat to her car and watch it from there. Being an independent woman on holiday alone, she had no-one else's plans to consider.

Yesterday had been fantastic. The beach below could only be accessed by descending steep, treacherous steps cut into the rock itself, dropping for a hundred and fifty feet before you reached the fallen jumble of boulders and the grey, gritty sand. It was the only place on the island, apart from the sandbar, where you could paddle in shallow water. And that was as much as you could do; even from the beach you could see strange currents and fast-flowing eddies caused by sharp rocks just below the surface. Sometimes the eddies joined into a sucking vortex, and you would glimpse seaweed-covered rocks as the sea withdrew, like skin being pulled back to disclose a view of rotting bones during nightmare surgery, before the sea's pulse hid them from view again.

There was also a cave, but she didn't explore far. She didn't like the feeling of enclosure and darkness, and could imagine the weight of rock above her crushing down, smothering. She'd found it hard to breathe until she left the echoing blackness of the cavern and staggered back into the light.

That wasn't the only time something here had fascinated, but also frightened, her.

While setting up her tent last evening she'd heard a strange moaning, which made the hairs on the back of her neck prickle. At first it sounded like a child sobbing somewhere nearby, but she couldn't see anyone. After a minute's silence she heard it again, only this time it reminded her more of a lovely but neurotic dog she used to own, which whined or howled whenever the phone rang.

But instead of pleasant memories, last night this odd sound made her think of ghosts and banshees, and she had almost (only *almost*) wished there had been a man around. The noise seemed to come from out at sea. She had lain on her stomach and peered over the cliff's edge, making out dark points in the water, near some rocks exposed by the tide. Intrigued, she'd grabbed her binoculars and zoomed in. The noise came again and she tracked it to one of the points in the water, and realised it was a snout! Nearby was another which lowered, revealing a sleek head with huge dark eyes and tiny ear holes. Long white hairs grew above the eyes, and Megan recognised them as the grey seals she had been hoping to see ever since she'd read about the community of over a hundred that lived around the coast of Ynys Diawl.

Then an even greater surprise – the rocks weren't empty, but had over thirty seals on them! She had read that seals left the water to digest their food, lazing on rocks and playing. Some lay on their backs and appeared to be dead until they lifted their heads, eyes half-closed, to look at something, before letting their heads flop wearily back with a contemptuous snort. A few made low growling noises as they splashed in or out of the water, and she spotted two of their pups, with white coats, snuggling against the three hundred pound bulk of a parent. She watched engrossed for half an hour as the light faded.

The other fright was during the night, when she was woken in her tent by an eerie noise. It was a sort of shriek and a moan, and something darted off, still screeching. At first it sounded like a witch shooting off on a broomstick, but when she heard it again, and it had the same pattern, she realised it must have been a Manx shearwater: a rare, nocturnal ground-burrowing bird.

This morning she had eagerly added two more entries to her notepad of wildlife sightings, which now read:

Shag or Cormorant (??)

Oystercatcher

Pipit (meadow?)

Choughs

Dunlin or rock pipit?

Gannet

Pied wagtail (on ruined wall near village)

Humming bird hawk moth (wow!)

Grey seals (amazing!)

Manx Shearwater (sound only, at night, spooky).

With all the wildlife to see, and the pile of puzzle books in her car's glove-box, why would she ever need a man to make the holiday any better?

The rain was falling heavily by the time she got everything packed away and climbed into her chunky Land Rover Defender. She was glad she owned it – people might have sneered back in the city, but she was getting full use out of it here.

She edged the vehicle over the rough ground, bouncing in her seat in a way that made her feel sick and young at the same time, and then onto the cliff track which she followed round the north-eastern promontory past the cheerful red-and-white-banded lighthouse on her right. Surrounded by its low white walls it looked like a cross between a fairy cake with a single candle, and a playful castle. She planned to head to the cliff-edge picnic area just north of Glanmor Fach, which would mean crossing trackless rough ground for a while, but the Land Rover could take it. The views were worth the jostling.

Having been on the island for three days, she had already found her favourite spots. In fact, some had been personally recommended by the kind Lord of the island, John something-or-other, who had taken an interest in her trip – welcoming her, asking how long she was staying, what she did for a living and so on – then pointing out places where she might camp. He was a funny man, fastidiously dressed and shorter than her, but it was nice to have someone so interested. Apart from a foray for supplies, she had hardly been in the village.

This was her chance to get away from it all, to a place where the sky seemed bigger.

It wasn't really running away.

She loved nature, and leaving Warrington for a holiday shortly after she had split up with Nick was just a coincidence.

She should have known it would be a mistake to go out with another teacher at the school. He taught maths, she was the gym mistress. Her early days as a promising professional junior gymnast were behind her, and a PGCE allowed her to change career and teach what she loved to the (mostly spoilt) girls of St Jude's Catholic Girls' College.

He had cheated on her and she felt doubly betrayed, because it was one of her own sixth-formers he was sleeping with.

Why? Megan was athletic and had a small, tidy body; she thought she was fairly attractive. She worked hard but loved affection. She was intelligent, and could speak German, French and Spanish (as well as English). She admitted that she could be quick-tempered sometimes, but couldn't everyone?

Her conclusion was this: she was thirty years old; Janine was seventeen.

Men. She was better off on her own.

After the bumpy ground beyond the lighthouse it was good to be on the small track again. She pulled up near a solitary, worn picnic table twenty feet from the edge of the cliff, and yanked the handbrake a touch more aggressively than was necessary.

The rain beat heavily on the windscreen, obscuring the view. She certainly wasn't going to leave the Land Rover yet, just to take it in. She shuffled through the assorted maps, books, leaflets and chocolate bar wrappers on the seat next to her until she found *100 Super Puzzles!*, with a biro lodged between the pages she'd reached.

She spent a while searching for words in a grid of letters, chewing the pen tip, but the perpetual downpour drumming on the Land Rover roof made her feel drowsy. She put the puzzle book down and her head back. A small siesta would be good for her. She engaged the central locking before she closed her eyes.

"You got the goods without incident?"

"Yes," said Osian, scowling. "Like usual. Then me and Seimon took over for trussing. All sacked up. Tidy, it was."

Seimon stood nearby, fidgeting, his fat mass visible in Lord John's peripheral vision.

"Good. Are you okay, Seimon?"

"Aye, just hot."

"You do look a bit red. Come here."

Seimon stepped over nervously. He wore a brown tweed jacket that he had given up trying to fasten across his expansive stomach. Lord John noticed beads of sweat on his bald head. He used his thumb to pull down one of Seimon's lower eyelids, examining the membrane beneath, then the eyeball, while Seimon looked up.

"Hmm. And the skin rash?"

Seimon removed his jacket and unfastened a grimy shirt cuff so he could pull up the sleeve. A red suppurating rash covered the inner elbow. Lord John glanced over it.

"Larger, isn't it?"

Seimon nodded.

"But it doesn't hurt at all?"

"No," replied Seimon. "I don't even notice it most o' the time."

"The picture of health you are," Osian joked sourly.

Lord John ignored Osian and smiled at Seimon with the manner of a reassuring doctor. "Good. Don't worry about it. It's just mild psoriasis. It will clear up before you know it. But there is work to be done now. You have still got the blood up at the school?"

"Aye. In the fridge. It's clotted in the bottles."

"Good. You go and get Wil. Drive to the boundary locations I told you about and spread it there. Make sure you use the same amount at each boundary stone. Clear?"

"Yes."

"And be quick. We have the special service later. You must be back for that."

"I will be."

"Good. Now go."

Seimon nodded and left the room. The front door slammed moments later.

Lord John turned to Osian, who stared back with his intense, deep-set eyes. His hair was coarse and threaded with grey like fine wires, as were his bushy eyebrows, divided by a frown line. Osian's skin was a weathered brown, and so lined by forty years' of outdoor life that he looked old. "Where are they?"

Without replying, Osian pushed away from the crumbling plaster of the wall he had been leaning on, and walked over to a door beneath the staircase. Lord John followed him across the threadbare carpet, trying to ignore the dire condition of the house because there were more important things to concentrate on.

Osian opened the door, releasing air that smelt of mildew. The understairs area was small and dusty. Osian gestured at two full sacks propped against the far wall, fastened tightly at the tops.

"Which is the ram?"

Osian pointed at the larger sack. It bulged and fell as the contents moved. Muffled and panicky sounds emanated from it. Osian stepped in and kicked the sack with a heavy boot. A groan escaped.

"Osian, you will need help. Perhaps get Iwan. Then take this one to the tomb, and the other to the chapel. Don't allow any outsiders to see. And keep it from the ewes – that goes without saying. You have done well."

Osian nodded, glaring down at the sack, which was curled into a shivering foetal shape. He spat on it. "Mancunians," he muttered.

Lord John patted him on the shoulder, then noticed a red patch of sore-looking skin was just visible, spreading from beneath Osian's hair. Osian still hadn't looked up, so Lord John wiped his hand on his trouser leg with a look of distaste.

She woke with a start.

The rain was still belting down, but on the border between consciousness and sleep was the echo of another noise which could have been a muffled shout, or a bark, or a bang. She'd felt a movement too, but it might have just been the sensation of falling that sometimes startles us awake.

Maybe it was thunder.

She yawned and stretched and picked up the book which had slipped from her knees in slumber. Then she wiped condensation from the windows and peered out, but it was as she expected – blurred cliffs with grey sea beyond, battered picnic table, smeared woods thirty feet away.

The view looked somehow different.

She grabbed her turquoise cagoule from the back seat, fastened it on and put the hood up, giving herself a pointy-headed appearance. Head protected and loins suitably girded, she out of her side of the Land Rover, facing the sea, and examined the vehicle while the blustery wind buffeted her.

The back end was lower than it should be, and, on examining more closely, she saw that the rear right tyre was flat.

Cursing, she glanced at the other tyres, which seemed okay. She went back to the flat one and squatted. Couldn't see any obvious cause of a puncture, so it was possible she had driven over something on her way here, and had acquired a slow puncture then. Or maybe it had gone at once (if that was possible) and that was what had woken her? She stared at the puzzling tyre, as if willing it to explain itself. Unlike her pupils, it remained silent.

It didn't matter. She'd have to try and change it, and no doubt get soaked in the process, and have damp clothes with no way to dry them. There was no point waiting until it stopped raining; by the time that happened it might be dark.

A glimpse of red in the woods – then it was gone. She saw it for a second only, but it left the impression of a big man in a red cloak or coat, hiding behind a tree.

Ridiculous. There was no-one there.

Nonetheless she kept her eyes on the woods for a full minute, despite the rain. She could see nothing suspicious now, but felt as if she were being watched. The edge of the wood was disconcertingly close. Close enough for someone to mess with her wheel and sneak back?

She needed to change the tyre and stop imagining things.

Opening the rear door, she rummaged for the jack and the toolbox. She closed the door and undid the spare tyre from the back of the Land Rover.

Was that a furtive movement in the trees?

Trying to hurry, she had trouble even getting the jack in place, especially since she didn't like to look away from the woods, to actually see what her hands were doing. The jack slipped, scratching the paintwork above the wheel, and she cursed again.

There *was* movement. Further along now.

She almost wept when the dog came running out of the woods, a huge black Labrador. It came bounding over. She dropped the tools and held her arms out, saying encouraging things, and the dog happily rushed to her to be fussed – she was so relieved that she didn't mind hugging the wet and muddy animal.

"Hi there," she said, "aren't you a good dog?" She examined the leather collar, after pulling out a twig lodged underneath it. A gleaming medallion was engraved with a name.

"Spotty, eh?"

The dog tilted its head to one side and wagged its tail even more.

"I'm glad you've come, you make me feel better already. You would watch out for nasty men for me, wouldn't you?"

She could only assume the dog was being walked. It didn't have the look or manner of a stray and it had a new collar.

Possibly the red shape she had glimpsed was the owner. Though where was he now?

She would walk the dog to the edge of the woods and see if the owner was there. She felt less nervous with the dog and wanted to make amends for her earlier cowardice. She was an independent woman, after all.

Hooking her fingers through his collar she squelched across the grass with Spotty, heading to where she had glimpsed the first movement, the flash of red.

"Hello?" she called, above the blowing wind.

There was no answer, but when she was within five feet of the first tree Spotty pulled back and started growling. She followed his gaze into the shadows, and slowly retraced her steps, attempting not to be pulled over by the frantically struggling animal.

As they cautiously withdrew the dog pricked up his ears and glanced at another point, where the path emerged from the wood near the picnic bench. Then she heard it too – a whistle, and shouting.

She retreated to her vehicle, alternating her attention between the two points, when a man emerged from the track. He was wearing a wet, blue tracksuit and something dangled from one hand. He spied her with the dog and jogged over, waving.

He didn't seem threatening, more happy to see them. And Spotty pulled towards him, wagging his tail. She kept hold of Spotty's collar though, as the man approached.

"Spotty, you *bad* boy, I've been looking everywhere for you!"

Spotty obviously wanted fussing so she let him go, and he ran to the man, who immediately clipped his lead onto the dog's collar and kept a firm hold on it.

He was perhaps younger than Megan, about six feet tall, slim and fit-looking. He was clean-shaven with short blonde hair, which was wetted down by the rain.

"Thanks for finding him, where was he?"

"It was more a case of him finding me. He came out of the woods and headed straight towards me."

"I'm sorry about that. He ran off, which is strange – he normally at least *pretends* to be obedient. I've been whistling and calling him for ages. Sorry if he disturbed you."

"It's fine, really. I'm glad he came. I was a bit spooked to be honest. I fell asleep in the car and woke with a flat tyre; then I thought I saw someone in red in the woods over there. Spotty had been growling at that spot too, just before you appeared."

The man glanced where she pointed, eyes searching the tree-line anxiously.

"What is it?" Megan asked.

"Well, it's just that Spotty was growling at something when he was with me too. Probably nothing," he added quickly with a surface smile of reassurance. "Did you fix your tyre?"

"No, I was having trouble."

"Well, tell you what, I'll give you a hand with it, and we'll have it changed in no time. In exchange, would you mind running me and Spotty back to the village? I'm soaking, and it would be miserable walking back."

"Okay, it's a deal."

"Can I put Spotty in your car now? I don't want the crazy sod running off again. We could put him in the rear compartment, he's pretty muddy I'm afraid."

"Sure."

She opened the rear door and moved the tent and camping equipment to one side. The four fold-down seats were already closed up, out of the way, and Megan unrolled the floor protector sheet before letting Spotty jump in. When they closed the door he continued to look out at them, hot breath misting the glass and nose smearing it.

"Why is he called Spotty?" Megan asked as they changed the tyre, still keeping one eye on the trees. "He doesn't seem to have any spots. He's just a black Labrador."

"Oh, that's my nephew's fault. When I first got the puppy he insisted on calling it Spotty. The name stuck, and I dropped my planned name of 'Killer'. Kids, eh, you just can't understand how their minds work."

"You weren't really going to call him Killer?" laughed Megan. "He's soft as butter."

"Well spotted. No, I was going to call him Rex."

Once the tyre was changed they got into the vehicle, Megan shifting all her bits from the passenger seat first. She let the hood down on her cagoule and re-tied her shoulder-length brown hair with a bobble before starting the engine.

"I appreciate the lift, especially since I'm dripping all over your seat. David Smithwick, by the way," he said, holding out his hand. "Or Constable Smithwick."

Megan shook it. "Megan Norris. A policeman?"

"Yes. New to the island. My predecessor's still in post, but I'll be the sole officer before long."

"That's why you seem trustworthy, then. So is Spotty your police dog?" She reversed the car – it took a few seconds to gain purchase: the grass was quickly getting sodden.

"Not really a police dog. He's a dog *owned* by a policeman; a dog who refuses to be trained to come back to heel when he smells a rabbit. It's probably my fault for bringing him up in a city. The smells here are just too exciting for him."

They drove along the track by the woods. And although he spoke with assurance, David kept watching the dark spaces under the trees, apparently glad to be leaving them behind.

They were just east of Glanmor Fach and heading south when they hit the girl.

The youth in the chapel was about sixteen years old. Scruffily dressed, with dirty hands and a few thick hairs growing unheeded from his chin. He wore an old pair of grey trainers splitting at the seams. He looked down respectfully when Brân Ddu spoke.

"*Fel 'na ma' hi. Hogyn da wyt ti, Joshua. Dw i eisiau i ti ddeud wrtha am bopeth glywi di.*" ["That is the way it is. You are a good boy, Joshua. I want you to tell me whatever you hear."]

The youth did not seem surprised that a girl not much older than himself would call him a boy. It was as if he accepted her superiority without question.

"*A 'nhad, os glywith o 'mod i'n deud wrthach chi?*" ["And my dad, if he finds out I tell you?"]

"*Breuddwydiwr braf 'dy dy dad, Joshua. Gofala di na fydd o'n deffro o'i freuddwydion.*" ["You have a nice dreamer for a dad, Joshua. Just make sure you don't let him wake up from his dreams."]

He grinned as she traced her fingertips gently down his neck and across his shoulders, feeling the rough knit of his jumper. He leaned towards her stroke eagerly, but she withdrew her hand.

"*Dos, a chofia beth ddwedais i.*" ["Go, and remember what I said."]

"*Iawn, Brân Ddu.*" ["I will, Brân Ddu."]

Once he had left, the young woman knelt in front of the chapel altar. The wooden floor was hard under her knees. There was a large crucifix on the wall ahead of her – but she never cared for *that*. She ran fingers through her wild hair, straightening out knots, unshadowing her pale and disturbingly beautiful face.

The chapel had a clean line of sight from the entrance to the altar, with panelled box pews on each side of the aisle. At the ends of the pews were carved faces entwined with oak boughs. The motif was repeated on the altar, and the girl delicately touched a curve between a carved oak leaf and a bunch of acorns growing out of the Green Man's head. Her finger slid back a hidden panel with a dry scrape.

She lifted out a cushion reverently. There was a black silk drape over it, which covered a large, irregularly-shaped object, all bumps and edges. She placed it in front of her on the floor, contemplating it for some minutes. Then she removed the drape, revealing a strangely-shaped bone. Sharp teeth edged one part, and it was almost two feet long.

A gust of wind rattled the round-arched stained glass windows and disturbed the candles, making them flicker, and she looked up with an expression that was a strange mix of wariness and exultation on her oval face. Through the windows she could see the shadows of the dark green yews outside swaying like mourners, yews said to be a thousand years old. Many things could live for a long time.

She leaned forward and kissed the bone. Her lips brushed it softly, and the tip of her tongue emerged from between them and caressed a contour of it lovingly.

Resting her ear against the bone, she listened.

The Girl

> "If I find shelter in the woods, and sleep in some thicket, I may escape the cold and have a good night's rest, but some savage beast may take advantage of me and devour me." – Homer, *The Odyssey*

The sky lit up for an instant, then darkened back to grey. Four seconds later there was a rumble of thunder. Rain sheeted down, and it was dark as dusk, even though it was only late afternoon. Visibility was bad but low-beam showed the muddy track clearly enough to stay on it.

The track was right up against the wood, so close that branches clawed at the windscreen. One second there was nothing; the next a surprised, pale face was caught in the headlights, just before the edge of the Land Rover struck the girl's hip and sent her spinning into a bush. Megan screamed and swung the steering wheel to her left, pushing hard on the brakes. The Land Rover skidded to a halt just off the track. She sat shaking and clutching the steering wheel.

"Are you okay?" asked David, unfastening his seatbelt. When she didn't answer he asked again, more insistently; this time she nodded blankly.

He jumped out into the rain and splashed to where the girl lay. The Land Rover was facing away, so the bushes were lit with an eerie red glow from the tail-lights. The girl had landed in thick hazel in such a way it looked as if she were reclining.

"Hello? Can you hear me?" he asked as he approached. "If you can hear me open your eyes."

There was no response. However, he could see she was breathing, and a quick check showed there was nothing obviously broken or dislocated. He hoped she had just been clipped.

Land Rover door slam; a presence behind him.

"Oh my God, is she all right? I didn't see her coming out of –"

"It's okay, Megan, I know. Give me a hand, we'll move her to your backseat. We probably shouldn't, but it would be worse to leave her like this until we get help."

They struggled to manoeuvre the girl. She was young, maybe only sixteen, with long, sandy, pink-streaked hair and an upturned nose, dressed in hipster jeans, canvas shoes and a tight top, which was soaking. David avoided staring at the girl's nipples, which stood out from her small breasts. There was the start of a bruise and swelling on the part of her right hip that showed above the jeans.

Opening the rear door, Megan ordered Spotty to lie down in the corner, then she lowered two fold-down seats and threw a blanket over them. She helped David to move the girl in, and as they lay her down the girl's eyes fluttered, then she sat up, wincing as she did so and putting a hand to her hip.

"It's okay, just lie back," said David.

"You came out of nowhere, I couldn't brake in time," Megan stammered.

"Where's Ken he wasn't – oh hell, what am I doing in car – oh." The girl's words sounded slurred and confused.

"Possible concussion," David whispered to Megan, who put a hand over her mouth, eyes widening in concern.

The girl rambled, apparently delirious. David could only make out the words "Ken" and "tent" as he tried to calm her. Suddenly the girl snapped, "Shut the fuck up, I'm okay!"

David and Megan shut up.

The girl looked around, clarity back in her eyes. She hissed in pain as she moved her leg. "You hit me with the car, right?"

"Yes," replied David. "You ran out of the woods in front of us. How do you feel?"

"Like crap. My hip's as sore as shit."

"Do you mind if I check? I'm a police officer."

From the periphery of his vision David saw Megan nodding to the girl.

"Okay." The girl raised herself up on her elbows and pulled her jeans down even lower, revealing the white strap of a thong.

David gently felt around the hip's curve. The girl made no noise but bit her lower lip. Her skin was cold around the swollen bits, but hotter on them. He pressed as gently as he could, while still following the line of bone. There were no irregularities as far as he could tell. A few of her sandy pubic hairs showed above the jeans.

"I think you're going to have a hell of a bruise, but hopefully nothing is broken," he said, sitting back.

The girl immediately readjusted her jeans, and moved to a sitting position, despite David's protests. She succeeded with only a few grimaces.

"We need to get you to a hospital now," said David.

"No!" she snapped. "We have to find Ken first."

"Ken?"

"My boyfriend. I'm not going anywhere without him."

"Where is he?"

"I don't know, or I'd be with him, right? He's missing someplace in these fuckin' woods."

"Maybe he wandered off somewhere, to use the toilet."

"Don't patronise me! I know the difference between Ken going for a shit and Ken going missing. There's really something weird going on here."

She caught the anxious glance between David and Megan, and interpreted it as disbelief. "I'm telling you it's true!" she yelled, getting their attention back. Then, in a lower voice, "We were camping in the woods here, right? Near a clearing. About an hour ago he went for a piss, just in some bushes near our tent, and he was talking to me about something – some joke from a rubbish sci-fi film he'd seen – while he was peeing. I was packing stuff up so we could stay in the tent for the rest of the day, or until the pissing rain let up, not fully listening to him, because he always bores me with those nerdy films he watches. And one second he was telling me this joke, and I was waiting for the punch line: and it never came. Just silence. I went and looked – he wasn't there. I assumed he was hiding, being a prick, and said I wasn't amused. But after a bit it was so weird that I got really scared and angry, and shouted that if he didn't come out from wherever he was hiding it would be over between us, for real. And he didn't come out. There is no *way* he wouldn't have done if he was there, because he *knows* when I'm serious about something. He wouldn't play a trick on me like that. So I started to lose it. I felt like there was something really bad-shit going on. I was looking for him and got lost and ran out here when I saw lights and heard an engine. I need help."

David said, "I think the best thing we can do is get back to the village for help, then we can –"

"You're not listening to me, I said we need to go and look for him NOW! He might need help NOW. I'm not going anywhere without Ken, I'm really worried and I am asking for help right now, and you're a policeman, that's your job isn't it, helping people?" Her sharp eyes cut through David – he felt them slicing him so keenly that he swallowed and looked down.

"Okay," he said softly. Then, turning to Megan, "Drive us into the clearing, along the track from the south. It should be wide enough, and you'll have no problem with the terrain in a vehicle like this. We'll toot the horn, see if he comes – then think about what to do next."

He climbed into the passenger seat and Megan pulled back onto the track, driving slowly around the edge of Glanmor Fach.

"What's your name?" asked David.

"My name's Patricia, but don't call me that. I prefer Patti. Like Patti Smith."

"Okay, Patti. I'm Constable Smithwick."

She wrinkled her small nose at his formality.

David unclipped his mobile phone from under his tracksuit top. He was glad the case was waterproof.

Patti leaned over and saw what David had. "Oh great, you've got a phone!"

"Don't get your hopes up too much," said David. "I haven't had more than two bars since I got here, and most of the time I'm lucky to get one. I only have it with me out of habit. See – nothing."

He tried dialling the police station in the village, then Constable Huws' home number, but there wasn't even a tone. He put it away in disgust. A phrase of Lord John's popped into his head, something the Lord had said in David's first week here: "There are no cancer-causing mobile phone masts on *this* island, Officer."

He would have been willing to take the risk of cancer right then.

When they reached the track through Glanmor Fach, Megan put the Land Rover's lights on main beam and edged the vehicle into the woods. The driving was nerve-wracking. The last thing he wanted was to get stuck *here*.

They reached the clearing where David had first lost Spotty. "Circle round, use the horn," he told her. "All of us keep our eyes peeled."

"Too bloody right," said Patti.

But the brooding trees kept their secrets in the rain.

After a few minutes Megan stopped using the horn, braked, and turned to David. "What now?"

He surreptitiously glanced at Patti's determined face in the rear-view mirror. A knot tightened inside him. "I'll get out. Look around a bit."

Patti said she'd go too.

"I don't want to be left alone!" snapped Megan.

"You'll be okay. I'll leave Spotty with you. I don't want him running off again anyway. You turn round and be ready to drive back with us when we return. With Ken."

Spotty had been silent in the back during the driving. The girl stroked him, and Spotty licked her fingertips.

"Can I have him in the front with me?" Megan asked. "I'd feel safer."

"Of course."

David and Patti got out and moved Spotty to the front seat, bringing the rich stink of wet dog hair with him.

"We should be back in ten minutes or so," David told her. He made a circular gesture with his hand, and she nodded as she put the window up, engaged the central locking, and turned the car round to face the exit from the clearing.

David confronted the dark wood. The trees seemed more twisted and menacing than he remembered.

"I appreciate this," said the girl.

"Sure."

They walked across the clearing. She limped but assured him she was okay. "It's no worse than the rain."

When they entered the greater darkness under the trees it took his eyes a minute to adjust, and he nearly tripped over a slippery, exposed root. They both moved quietly without having agreed to do so; as they left the clearing behind he noticed that Patti was edging closer to him.

No animal noises. Only the pitter-patter of water finishing the assault course through the big oak leaves and reaching the ground, dying with a final wet sound to mark its passing.

"The tent's over there, he wanted to be hidden from the road," Patti whispered, pointing beyond a fallen tree lying on the ground, covered in moss, and revealing its rotten, insect-eroded insides.

They heard a clatter. The view was blocked by dense bushes. Patti grabbed David's hand and held it tightly. Again the noise, like pans being rattled on the forest floor.

They crouched and inched forward. David noted that Patti wasn't calling out Ken's name. He was glad of that.

When they reached the bushes they both heard a groan, followed by a slap, and another moan.

Neither of them could hide their fear from the other.

He parted the branches of a bush (*quietly, oh so quietly*) so they could see better, and then wished he hadn't.

Patti crushed his hand. There were tears in her eyes. David knew that the man with the badly-bruised face, who was chained between two beech trees by his wrists in a crucified pose, must be her Ken.

Nearby a large man – definitely over six feet, but badly hunched over, and with solid-looking arms and upper body – was rummaging through a sports bag, throwing clothes onto the damp earth. The big man was dressed in a red plastic coat with the hood up, so they couldn't see his face.

He threw the bag onto the ground and slapped the chained man across the face hard. The chained man moaned but could hardly lift his head up.

Doing a quick calculation, David worked out that the man in the red coat probably outweighed him by up to five stone. He'd also spotted a large axe lying near the tent. He assumed it wasn't Patti's. David's throat was dry. He didn't fancy taking on the red-coated giant. But could he live with himself if he were to sneak back the way he had come and leave Ken to whatever the monster had planned?

The big man reached down and picked something up.

Oh God. It was a saw.

This wasn't pretend; this wasn't a game.

The huge man grabbed Ken's long rain-plastered hair in his left hand, put the saw blade just above the elbow of Ken's left arm, and began to saw with powerful cutting motions.

It all seemed to happen at once.

Ken started screaming. Blood spurted from his arm, and once it was cut through – after only a few strokes – he collapsed writhing on the ground with blood pouring from his stump, as the rest of his arm clattered into the opposite tree, still attached to its chain.

Patti stood up and screamed Ken's name while holding out her arms, as if she could help him.

The big man spun at her voice, blood slicking from his coat in the rain, and David glimpsed a horribly disfigured face. He was thankful he wasn't close enough to see exactly what was wrong with it.

The big man dropped the saw, picked up the axe in one hand, and limped his way quickly towards them.

David grabbed Patti's hand and ran back the way they had come, dragging her with him until she began to run on her own.

The big man was fast, but slowed by the limp. They could outrun him. However, it wasn't a great distance to the car – he wouldn't be far behind when they got there.

"That was Ken!" howled Patti. "Oh my God, that was Ken! He killed him!"

"Just fucking run!" David screamed back, focussing on the obstacles ahead. He let go of her hand so he could move quicker. She fell behind, but he couldn't waste thought on that. The ground was slippery and uneven, with brambles and roots to avoid. He could hear branches snapping as their pursuer came after them.

A shriek behind him. He glanced back, and Patti was sprawled on the leaves, trying to scramble up. He could run back a few feet, grab her and help, but he could also see red through the trees. They weren't far enough ahead. What to do? Her eyes begged him. All in one, two, three fast heartbeats, he panicked and ran on – *she would be fine* – his heart racing, then a struggle and a scream behind him, oh God ...

He ran across the clearing yelling at Megan to start the engine; she did so, probably because she saw his panic rather than because she heard his words. He jumped in beside her yelling, "Go! Fucking drive, we've got to go now!" She floored the accelerator while he watched for pursuit.

"Where's Patti?"

"There's a killer there, he got her before I could do anything, just watch where you drive for God's sake!" Spotty was barking, and David yelled at him to shut up. He wiped his eyes with the back of his hand, trying to hide his face from Megan; it was just rain running down his face, just rain, he'd done all he could.

They left the wood.

"Follow the track back to the village, we'll be safe there," he commanded. Megan was silent.

"Not too near the trees! Keep on the far side of the track or leave it altogether if you have to!" His eyes flicked amongst the trees as he grabbed his phone again, but he already knew he wouldn't get any help that way.

The pale, beautiful young woman strode angrily up the main street back to her house.

She was being excluded. Excluded from information. From *His* plans. She had only just found out about the takings; and that everyone from the logging camp was dead. Brân Ddu gritted her teeth at that.

She was also being excluded from the rituals, which was a sacrilege – *she* was the one able to channel power. When she gave herself to someone they received power from her, communion of the body. And in return she was filled with power, the receptacle for the dark energy. She was special. She should always be first. Without her the ceremony was an empty thing.

Instead, on His orders, the men had dragged in some other woman they had caught. Someone *unwilling.* That wasn't the way it was meant to work. But *He* wanted a different ceremony, which only the men, and that victim, would attend.

She didn't like to be excluded. She was the Harbinger, the Black Crow, sacred to the Furies, priestess of the darkness within. To be sent away from her place, by *Him* ...

She was not happy, and the rain soaked into the black cardigan she pulled tightly round her body.

The Old Man

> "Beneath this face that appears so impassive Hell's tides continually run" – Walt Whitman, *You Felons On Trial In Courts*

The Land Rover roared into Pentref Bychan and jerked to a halt in front of the small building that acted as a police station, opposite the village pub.

The settlement seemed deserted.

"Come with me into the police station. No, leave Spotty there for now. He'll be fine."

They rushed into the building. David had only vaguely explained what had happened. And Megan didn't want to know the details.

"Constable Huws! Emyr!"

David checked both the downstairs rooms they used as the police station but there was no sign of the other officer, even though the front door hadn't been locked.

Next he went through to the back to get his hand-held police radio, which was powerful enough to connect him to the mainland regardless of weather or conditions. But where it should have been in the locked cabinet was only a blank space.

"It's gone!" he said, then kicked a chair over in frustration and looked around the room.

Megan seemed somehow paler, despite her tanned skin, as she silently watched him with wide eyes. Hope must be made of colour.

He was getting distracted. He had to think clearly.

The other option was the landline. The phone was surrounded by coffee-cup circles where Constable Huws always left his morning drink, but when David lifted the grimy, cream-coloured receiver, there was no dialling tone. He tried his mobile, but still couldn't get a signal.

"Fuck! We can't contact the mainland from here."

"What about the pub? We could get help there," suggested Megan.

"Okay, come on."

But when they got outside David paused. "Wait here."

"Why?"

"I just want to get something. I'll be less than a minute."

He ran back along the road, past the village shop with old signs in the window for "Rhug Estate Pork Sausages" and "Davies' LOSSIN DANT HOME Quality Welsh Mints", back to the row of terraced houses, of which David's was the first. His windows reflected the grey sky back at him above their rotten wooden ledges.

He unlocked the front door and charged into the hall, flung open the understairs cupboard, and rooted through the contents before dragging out a heavy red suitcase. He rotated the dials of its combination lock to 9-9-9 then flicked the catch, opened the case and rummaged through blankets and old clothes until his hand closed on what he sought.

He cradled it. His guilty secret.

It was a French Lebel double-action revolver with a hexagonal barrel, and although it was light, it *felt* reassuringly heavy in his hands as he held the worn brown grip. He opened the cylinder and checked that all six chambers were loaded.

It was old – early twentieth century, possibly even used in the First World War. The textured grip ended in a rusting metal hoop by which an officer had perhaps attached the pistol to his uniform. Above the handle one could just read:

M^{re} *d'Armes*

St *Etienne*

and the pistol's serial number. It was easy to imagine it being fired by an officer as he climbed out of a trench to storm the enemy line.

The pistol had belonged to a petty thug in a city gang. David had recovered the weapon after the thug, escaping, had shoved it into a bin as he ran past, obviously hoping no-one would notice. David didn't know how such a museum piece had got into the gangster's hands, but it had ended up in his.

And instead of turning it in, he had kept it, even though it was a sackable offence. An impulse. No-one else had seen him take it, and the thug obviously hadn't told the other officers that he'd been carrying a gun.

David knew it was wrong. He knew it made him a dishonest officer. Yet he had been messed up since Officer Clavin's fatal stabbing a few weeks previously. He hadn't been sleeping. Before every shift he had a cold sweat that he hid as best he could. And when he realised the person he had been chasing had been armed, and had, thankfully, thrown the gun away instead of turning and using it ...

Not long after that he had put in for the transfer.

And the impulse that had led him to keep the gun originally led him to keep it still. He found he slept better with it in the house, even though it was hidden.

He was glad of that impulse now. And glad the pistol still worked; he had finally plucked up the courage to test it in the cellar of his Swansea home. Getting more working ammunition had been a challenge, but not insurmountable. He slipped it into the pocket of his tracksuit bottoms, and the five spare 8mm rounds went into the other pocket.

As he moved back to the front door he thought for a second he heard a creak from upstairs. He looked up the steep staircase which merged into shadow. Was it the house protesting at his rushed entry and banging? Well, it could have peace again. He had to get back to Megan.

They dashed over the road, only stopping to get Spotty out of the car. David kept him on a tight lead as they ran through pounding rain to Yr Hen Ddyn.

Megan expected people and conversation but the pub was empty and in darkness.

"Hello? Is anyone there?" David asked. No answer.

Megan didn't feel like suggesting they should search the whole building. Her instincts told her it would be empty. She headed over to the bar and tried the phone there. "Dead," she reported.

David nodded but said nothing.

She took a tumbler from behind the bar. Her hands were shaking but she managed to pour a glass of some dusty-labelled Welsh spirit she'd never heard of, then took a fiver from her purse and left it sticking out from under an ashtray. She stood sipping the sweetly-pungent liquid in silence, stroking Spotty with one hand. She hadn't thought that the bottom could fall out of the world so quickly.

The room was rectangular. The double-doored entrance faced the bar. To the right were a fireplace and a door to the toilets and staircase. Open space was broken up by dark chairs and a couple of large wooden tables with flaking varnish. Behind the bar were two more doors. To have something to do, David tried them. One was locked, while the other opened into a storeroom, which led to the yard at the back. No noise but rain on glass. It was getting dark.

Megan finished her drink. "Maybe we should try and drive to the mainland?" she suggested. "Get help there?"

"But we shouldn't need to!" David snapped, exasperated. "Where is everyone? There must be a logical explanation!" He eyed the bottles behind the bar then gritted his teeth and began pacing. He'd done two laps when they heard footsteps pounding up to the pub door. David spun around as the door opened, his hand going to his trouser pocket, and a man in a polo shirt and shaved head stepped into the bar. He glanced dismissively from David to Megan, stamped water from his shoes, and began to walk across the room.

"Who are you?" David asked with an edge to his voice.

The man stopped, then slowly turned. "Chris Jones." He stared at David.

"What are you doing here?"

"Staying here, mate. Going upstairs to dry off. Nice to meet you." He glanced at Megan, and added: "Both."

He was about to move on when David asked, "Have you seen anyone else around? Or anything strange?"

The man gave a forced smile. "I haven't seen anyone for a while, no. Probably because I've been walking in pissing rain, and everyone with more sense than what I've got is somewhere warm and dry with a cup of tea. The only strange thing I've seen is you, mate, asking a stranger questions when he obviously wants to go to his room to put some dry clothes on. Excuse me."

Chris turned and left the room, and this time David didn't stop him.

"What does that mean?" asked Megan. "And why didn't you get him to help?"

"Help? How?" David's voice was harsh. "Get him to go back to the woods with me? No chance. Get him to fix the phones? Tell him about a murder and create a panic? Ask him to tell me where everyone is, when he doesn't know? Think, will you! He's probably right. We've got a serious situation but people are around somewhere. There's an explanation. Maybe we'll just drive to the mainland as you say. But first I should at least try and find the other officer, and warn some of the villagers, so people can stay safe indoors. I'll find a few responsible people, even if I have to knock on every door in the village. But I won't go blabbing to the first stranger I meet, okay? So maybe let me do the thinking, and just ..." He sighed when he saw Megan was sobbing into Spotty's fur. "I'm sorry, Megan. It will be fine."

"It doesn't feel fine."

David turned the pub lights on, banishing the oppressive darkness. Megan blinked until her eyes adjusted to the new yellowness. "See, things look better already."

Megan didn't laugh.

The chapel bell began to ring. David froze, then let out a breath.

"Of course! What an idiot! There's probably a service going on. We'll wait here a bit longer – some of the men will come here when it's over. We'll warn people then get going. It's the best plan I can think of."

Chris ascended the stairs to the L-shaped landing. His room was at the back, next to the bathroom, but he didn't go there straight away. He sat on the big window ledge at the front of the pub, in darkness, staring out at the gloom.

Chris hadn't recognised the woman, but he knew the guy was a copper, which is why he didn't want to hang around down there. It wasn't so much that the copper would recognise him and link him to anything, but he might ask questions; questions often lead to more questions, and if he was a suspicious type he might check up on some of the answers. Then Chris would have to move on, and anyone looking for him would have more clues to his movements.

When the chapel bell began to ring he looked out of the window, thoughts interrupted. With his forehead against the cold glass he could see the edge of the chapel and some of the graveyard. He wanted to get out of his wet clothes but was intrigued by the first signs of humanity, outside the world of the pub, that he'd come across since he'd reached the logging camp.

The bell rang a few times, irregularly, then the last echoes faded out. He could see the setting sun, burning red behind the Celtic cross on a hill in the graveyard.

By the chapel was light. He rubbed condensation away, and looked again. The light was the beams of electric torches, carried by a few of the twenty or thirty men from the village walking up the main street from the chapel. The pub was the first building they would reach.

He was curious now. Where were they going in such a big group? He assumed it wasn't usual for the whole congregation to go to a pub straight from the chapel.

When the group got closer it halted. The torches flicked off one by one. The group continued forward towards the patches of light that spilled out of the pub windows and halfway across the road.

Only as they approached the pub doors did he notice the villagers seemed to carry objects that gleamed in the weak light.

Downstairs, Spotty growled in the direction of the pub entrance. Megan, sitting by the bar with him, clutched his lead tighter. David followed Spotty's intense stare, then backed away from the door, knocking a stool over in the process, which he ignored. He trusted the dog.

Just as he reached Megan the door opened and villagers surged in.

It seemed at first as if none of them spoke, but then David noticed that while some wheezed asthmatically, others were muttering. He couldn't make out anything comprehensible from the slurred sounds. Even without their sinister and jerky shuffling, David would have known something was wrong. The eyes of all the men struck him as being somehow dead. Not only were they glazed, but he could make out something sticky-looking around Wil Griffiths' eyes, the ginger-haired man who ran the garage and was at the front of the group.

Most of the men were carrying weapons – in Wil's hand was a rusty bar; someone behind him had a worn sickle; the tall skinny barman, Iwan, was carrying a knife and a length of rope. Peredur Morgan, dressed in his usual fish-smelling, worn jumper, could sometimes be counted on for a few taciturn words when he came back from fishing and crabbing on the rocks, selling what he didn't eat in the village. However, now he just stared, while one twitching hand held a heavy cudgel, and the other a tangled net.

David wasn't taking any chances and, trying to control the tremor in his hand, he snatched the revolver out of his pocket and aimed it at the men, who were advancing straight towards him. Megan glanced in panic at the handgun. David gestured to get behind the bar, which she did, dragging the growling dog with her.

"Stay back everyone!" David shouted. "Peredur, Iwan, what are you doing? Put those weapons down."

He followed sideways after Megan, who was panicked enough to keep moving. She pushed open the door at the end of the bar and darted into the storage room, looking for an exit. Good girl, thought David.

"This is my last warning!" he said. He was almost at the door himself. There were already about fifteen people piling into the pub, and more outside. Two men were at the end of the bar, following him and staring glassily. His attention on them for a second, he almost missed the lunge as Iwan leaned fully across the bar in front of him and slashed with his knife. David leapt back just in time, crashing into the shelves behind the bar. Bottles rolled off, smashing on the floor. As Iwan pulled back his hand to strike again, almost lying across the bar, David pistol-whipped the side of his head hard and dashed past. Iwan's knife rattled to the floor, but even as David followed Megan into the storeroom he saw Iwan standing up, unfazed by the hard blow he had just received to the temple, muttering, "*Ci tew, mochyn tew, ci tew, mochyn tew* ..." ["Fat dog, fat pig, fat dog, fat pig ..."]

David slammed the door shut. The villagers were only seconds behind them. The room contained shelves of dusty bottles, cloths, and aged packets of crisps. More boxes, broken furniture and wooden barrels littered the floor. A small window looked out over the yard behind the pub.

Megan was rattling the back door handle. "It's locked!" she screamed. "There's no key!"

"Smash the window!" he yelled back, trying to drag a barrel in front of the door they had come through to buy a few seconds. Spotty was barking, adding to the chaos.

The villagers pounded on the door and David leaned against it, but he couldn't hold it for long. Megan grabbed a broken stool from under a cloth and swung it at the window. Glass shattered outwards into the yard. One vicious shard remained stuck up in the frame, so she knocked it out with the stool before flinging it aside.

The door by David's head splintered as part of a meat cleaver split the wood. He let the door go. Megan was scrambling out of the window. David grabbed Spotty, and threw him out as well. The door flew open behind him, the barrel scraping to one side. David fired at the first man to come through, then two more shots into the half-open door itself to hit whoever was first behind it.

He didn't recognise the person he had shot; the man took a bullet in the shoulder and spun backwards out of sight, dropping the meat cleaver somewhere outside the room. David grabbed splintered window frame and hoisted himself through, without cutting himself on any of the jagged pieces.

Luckily, the wide backyard gate was open. Megan was standing just outside the exit from the yard, looking back. Spotty dashed past her and disappeared, his black coat swallowed up by the twilight, only the rattle of his lead dragging on the ground giving a clue to his direction.

The men were filling the storeroom. In white rage David thrust the gun through the frame and squeezed off shots at point blank range. Deafening bangs; recoil pain shooting up his arm; body thrown against body without a cry; someone crashing over a barrel into a crate of bottles. The smell of burning; cold rain at his back; the fire of revenge and fear shooting from his fingertips; drops of blood splashing over the wall by the door; plaster flying from above the door frame. Then intense agony in his gun arm. The pistol fell into the room and David took two steps back, a sickle embedded through his forearm which burnt like fire, heat running down his arm. With his left hand he gripped the handle and yanked it out – there were patches of rusty discolouration on the blade; then the sickle fell amongst the broken glass, and he hugged his ripped and bleeding arm close to his body, and backed away from the window, crunching across glass.

Someone was climbing out of the window after him already. He sprinted from the yard and saw Megan in the gloom ahead, running towards the back of the garage. He followed.

Chris had watched the villagers enter the pub; had heard shouting, then things crashing. He didn't need to hear more.

He crossed the landing to his bedroom, which was unlocked. Iwan had refused to give him a key, saying there was no need – Chris had no choice in the matter but was glad now, since it saved him fumbling with keys in the dark. Once inside he gripped the wardrobe and heaved it over with a crash, so that it blocked the door. He rushed to his window, which looked onto the pub's backyard, and yanked it up. It was stiff, but he was strong, and after straining he eased it up enough to fit through the gap.

Heavy footsteps were coming up the stairs – more than one person.

Gunshots rang out below.

He climbed out of the window, lowered himself until he was dangling by his hands, then kicked away from the wall and let go. He fell over as he landed, his foot catching on a full bag of rubbish by a bin, and scrambled up, shaking bits of vegetables and something wet and stinking off his foot. The door to his bedroom above was being splintered. More gunshots.

The woman he'd seen in the pub ran through the gates out of the yard, and he took off in the same direction as her. She didn't even notice he was there; she was in a blind panic. Looking back, Chris saw the cop stagger out of the yard, holding his arm.

As Chris and the woman ran past the garage the copper caught up, yelling at the woman – Megan, apparently – to wait. She ignored him but Chris grabbed her arm, spinning her round, off balance. She looked at Chris; she was startled but recognised him. The copper caught up.

"We've got to get to my car!" said the woman. "We can drive away!"

"No!" said the copper. "We parked in front of the police station – opposite the pub. We'd have to run back down the main road, where they are. My car is right outside my house, just follow me."

He ran round the side of the garage, fumbling with his good arm for his keys.

Chris pulled the woman with him. She seemed dazed, but at least she kept up. Outside one of the houses was a Subaru Impreza, the cop's car. The copper dropped the keys, picked them up, and tried to unlock the door with his left hand. Chris could see that his right arm was badly injured, his tracksuit top dark red with blood where his wounded arm had been held against it as he ran. Through the rain he could also see people coming down the road towards them from the pub, running now. There would only be seconds.

"Your dog!" Megan yelled to the copper, suddenly snapping out of her fugue.

"He'll be fine, he can look after himself," the cop replied as he got the keys in; the doors unlocked with a whirr.

Chris shouted "Get in the back!" The copper was going to argue, but Chris could see he had lost a lot of blood and he didn't want him fainting from shock while driving them. "You're injured, just do what I say!" He elbowed the copper out of the way, snatched the keys and got into the driving seat. Key in the ignition and the engine roared into life first time. The woman was already climbing into the back and the copper realised he might get left behind, so jumped in too.

Thankfully, the vehicle was facing away from the pub. Chris slammed the car into gear, released the brake and, with a squeal of tyres, rocketed down the street, just as the back window exploded inwards and a shower of minute crystals of glass bounced over the cop and woman. A scythe blade was caught in the upholstery of the back seat. The man wielding it was dragged along for ten feet before he let go and rolled, lacerated, in the road. The scythe handle bounced off the ground, dislodging the blade, and that too clattered off onto the tarmac.

In the rear-view mirror Chris could see the villagers running after them. He flicked on the windscreen wipers and lights and focussed on the road.

Lord John crossed the garden of Plas Dof, the large house overlooking Pentref Bychan.

In a corner, by the high garden walls, was a clump of yew trees surrounding a marble mausoleum. Most of his ancestors had been entombed below it, sealed in forever. Do Gooders or Realists, it didn't matter in the end. Their bodies were metaphorical worm-food.

But the Ynyr Fychans decided they didn't want to lie forgotten, so they left means by which people could come and pray at their tomb – misguidedly and egotistically expecting that people would. The small man lifted a rusting grid in front of the mausoleum, crushing some large snails in the process. Others were stuck to the underside of the grid. He moved it to one side, into the long grass which was being pounded down in the rain.

The man lowered himself, and stood up to his waist in a square concrete hole, about two feet on each side, which the grid had covered. Then he turned on his torch. A yellow beam extended down to his feet. He knelt on the wet, slimy stones; around him snails and slugs were on the move. Other creatures disappeared into cracks when the light passed over them.

He crawled on his hands and knees along a claustrophobic tunnel below the ground. His shoulder nudged a snail, which fell with a crack, and his knee crunched the shell as he passed over. After a few feet he reached steps leading down to an echoing chamber and paused to brush the spiders' webs off his head. He was glad his body was compact.

The floor of the wedge-shaped room was wet, since water ran down the steps and pooled blackly at the narrow end. The rear wall was old brick, with occasional gaps left so people could peep through at the coffins and pay their respects.

Or not.

His torch shone on the hole he had made in the lower right of the wall by removing bricks. He crawled through that into a chamber beyond, where his ancestors had thought they would never be disturbed.

They would be disturbed tonight, though, that was for certain.

It smelt musty, with undertones of decay, damp, mould, urine and vomit. He took a lighter from his pocket and lit the candles he had placed in niches and next to coffins. One candle had been balanced in the eye socket of an ancestor whose coffin lid was open. Then he turned off the torch.

A muffled sound came from the corner. He carried a candle over, revealing a man chained by his wrists to a ring set in the moss-covered wall. The man was dressed in tracksuit bottoms and an FCUK T-shirt. A gold chain hung round his neck, and he had a gold hoop in each ear. His hair was cut short, flat on top, with tramlines round the sides. His face was bruised and his clothes damp and slimy; silver gaffer tape covered his mouth. He eyed the new visitor warily, and tried to say something but it just came out as "mmns" and "nnnghs".

"There is no point speaking to me. I can't understand you. Even without the gag, your Manchester accent was horrible, verging on incomprehensible. Anyway, I'm here now. Sorry you have had to wait, but at least you are no longer in a sack, eh? After all, you are important to me, and now is your time. The *only* time you will be useful in your pointless, ignorant life."

Lord John moved to a chest and opened it. The hinges protested with a squeal. He rummaged amongst the contents, which rattled and clanked together, then withdrew a foot-long rusty iron spike with a sharp point. He held the tip in front of the man's face, making him flinch away, but Lord John followed him, always holding the spike where the man could see it.

"Don't get too hopeful that the importance means you will be spared, though."

The man screwed up his eyes tight, refusing to look; Lord John jabbed it into the man's ear in one hard movement that forced the spike deep into the eardrum. The man immediately opened his eyes and jerked his head away, trying to scream. Lord John chuckled as blood welled out of his victim's ear and down his neck, staining the T-shirt.

"Don't shut your eyes on me again. I hate to be ignored. It's rude. Stop crying. You've still got another ear. I want you to hear me, don't I? But it is appropriate justice – you made an *awful* racket when you drove into my village in that souped-up car of yours. Dreadful loud bass noise and rap, or whatever the cacophony was. It hurt my ears," and here he leaned down to the tied-up man's good ear, and whispered in a friendly tone, "so I'm just showing you how it feels. Not nice, is it? Not nice to disturb the peace. Not nice to come here all cocky, with your muscles and noise, pretending you own the place. Some *primitive* like you, *own* the place? Own *my* island? You make me sick!"

He emphasised the last point by jabbing the man's stomach with the metal point. The man tried to move back but the wall blocked him. Spots of red bloomed on his T-shirt.

"See what you made me do?" Lord John threw the spike to one side and stood as it rolled to a halt in the corner. "Don't make me angry. I lose control sometimes. I do things I might regret. I don't want to waste your blood."

Lord John removed his clothes, placing them, neatly folded, on a mildewed coffin lying in a rectangular hole cut into the rock. Jacket and shirt first.

"You may be wondering what I am going to do."

He had noticed the look of fear as he took off his shoes and socks, then removed his trousers.

"Don't worry, my friend. It is nothing like *that*. I won't injure your fragile masculinity by going inside you. I don't know where you've been, do I? No, we used your mate for that – if that's what she was – in a very nice little ceremony at the chapel an hour ago. Please don't look so upset! We killed her afterwards, so she needn't be ashamed. Though I think she secretly enjoyed it. She was quite animated. Stop wriggling; the cords will only cut in deeper. You are not here for that. Nor for hunting. You look young and surprisingly fit, considering you probably live off McDonald's rubbish and cans of lager, and I'm sure you would give us a good run on a hunt. You would add a nice spice to the proceedings, and make a change from foxes or hares. Do you know, I have even resorted to hunting the sheep, from time to time. They now more-or-less run wild on the island. Dire straits indeed; they are completely rubbish, and it is over far too quickly, no matter how much of a head start you give them. And some just get cornered near the cliffs and fall off. Boring. But if there haven't been any drifters for a while, what can one do?"

He was now naked. He had a small, scrawny body, with a slightly distended stomach that was starting to sag. His face looked fairly young, but the greying hair suggested he was nearer fifty than thirty.

"No, I'm not going to be carnal with you. I just didn't want blood on my clothes. It's easier to wash off my skin. You see, I need you for this. My last sacrifice. My *personal* sacrifice, to fill me with darkness. Rather than being part of the general harvest you will feed the hunger in a special way. So I'm going to torture you to death. What do you think of that?"

The young man pulled at the chains as he had already done so many times before, but it was futile.

"Don't struggle, you will need your energy for trying to scream. Mmm, what to start with?" Lord John rattled amongst the contents of the chest again. He lifted out two small, rusty hoops, which looked like old rings. "So much pain from the past. Thumbscrews are under-rated, you know."

He replaced them, and instead carried over a metal cap and fastened it over the young man's head. He struggled, but it was attached eventually. In front of the prisoner's wide eyes were two sharp rivets, with wing nuts on the far side.

"My grandfather's invention. Eyescrews. Each turn of the nut takes them closer to the eyeballs. Eventually they puncture them

– and on through the optic nerve, if you *really* keep twisting the screws. Impressive, yes? And people said he was mad! Well, some people did, until he tied them up and disciplined them. Between you and me, he *was* mad of course – he thought his dead wife visited him at night, and had long, hairy fingers like spider legs which she brushed across his face when he slept. Mad as a hatter. But he did have a creative mind, as you see. Not that you will for much longer! Please stop crying and wriggling; it will do no good. You are lost. L-O-S-T. I don't mean to take away your hope or anything, but no-one will find you. Your car is already over a cliff, Allt-Wen, never to be seen again. It is just you and me, Lord of this island, and no-one will rescue you, or even find your body. The crabs will see to that."

Then Lord John removed preserving jars with hinged lids from the chest, and lined them up, lifting each metal catch so the lids were open. This was followed by a small cloth package which he unrolled on the damp cement floor. There was a coil of fine rubber tubing and an ancient scalpel with flaking red smudges on the handle. He also took out a roll of masking tape.

"This is how it will go. I'm not really going to torture you to death; that was a mean thing for me to say. I'm going to make a small incision in your arm and insert this tube into the radial artery, to start extracting your blood. If you struggle while I do it I'll tighten the eyescrews. The pain when they puncture your eyeballs would be excruciating – so staying still would be better for you. Then I'm going to extract six pints of blood, which should be sufficient. You can struggle *then*, since it will help me out by pumping blood more vigorously. Don't worry, you won't die from filling the jars! Oh no. Though I'll then get out the big plastic container that also needs filling, and you *will* pass out well before that's over. And you will die while unconscious as I extract your last pints, so I'll have to start pumping your legs. That's hard work, but you won't need to worry at that point. Or ever again! Sorry, I can't resist a little joke. Bearing all that in mind, if you can, it's back to the question: am I going to need the eyescrews?"

Lord John started work.

Abandonment

"The tidal movements here are complicated. Its flow is strong and fast. A brief moment during the spring tide is the only time you can get to the island." – Yuki Urushibara, *Mushishi 8*

"I'm Megan. Megan Norris."

"I would say pleased to meet you, but I think we all wish we weren't here," replied Chris.

"True. You said you were Chris Jones?"

"Yeah. Well remembered."

Megan would have liked to have given up on the paper tissues, they were almost useless at dealing with all the blood coming from the huge ragged gash in David's forearm, but they were the only semi-sterile thing in the car. She threw a sopping blood-soaked mess on the floor, then held a bundle of clean ones over the wound. A plastic bag was tied in place over that, with a long rag from the glove compartment. Good job she wasn't squeamish. The angry wound, and the blood on David's track-suit top and now all over her hands, would have made her sick otherwise.

David turned away, gritting his teeth. He looked pale.

"It's the best we can do for now." Megan pulled his sleeve back down. "We need to stop the blood and prevent it getting infected. Though that knife thing –"

"A sickle," murmured David.

"Yes, well – that would have been dirty. We'll need to get you to a hospital as soon as we can, so it can be cleaned properly."

David held his arm up against his chest to slow the bleeding, though he grimaced when he moved it.

"I heard shooting," said Chris.

"That was me. I had a pistol but lost it. Don't worry, I'm a police officer," David added.

Chris didn't reply. He just watched the moving section of road ahead as it flowed under the illumination of the car's headlamps.

"I'm Constable Smithwick by the way. David Smithwick."

"Hello, David."

"You're pretty quiet, Chris."

"Just keeping my eyes on the road. The weather is treacherous. We'll be at the sandbar in a minute, can cross to Anglesey, head for Beaumaris for help."

"That sounds good." David grimaced.

"But what's going on?" asked Megan. "What was wrong with them?" The draught from the broken back window made her shiver.

"It makes no sense," replied David. "I knew some of those people in the pub – and they tried to kill us! And the man in the woods ..."

"What man?" asked Chris.

David gave him a brief – and selective – version of the events earlier.

"That's all fucked up. Must be connected though. Too much of a coincidence otherwise."

"Well, we don't understand, and don't need to. It's a job for the rest of the police force. And we'll be leaving it in their capable hands before long."

Chris braked. "Or not," he said, flatly.

Where the sandbar should have been, was fast-flowing black water, rushing south in a channel between Ynys Diawl and Anglesey. Half a mile of dangerous, cold, churning water with unpredictable eddies separated them from the mainland. The car headlights reflected back as if from a lake of bubbling black tar. They all got out of the car to look. The rain was the least of their worries now.

"The tide is in," said Chris.

"Not quite," replied David hopelessly.

"Then where's the path across?"

"Gone."

"Gone? How can that be?" Chris demanded.

"Technically the tide should be out still. But the sandbar sometimes shifts around or disappears – it's basically an underwater sand dune, where stuff undercut from the cliffs is pushed into mounds on top of the bedrock. So at low tide you can cross it, because the water is shallower. But although the tides govern sea levels and are mostly predictable, the currents aren't, and they govern the sandbar. In a storm like this, even in shallow water, it may have moved or been breached. It will come back eventually when the currents settle down."

"Shit!" Chris thumped his palms against the car roof. "'Eventually' sounds a long time in the future."

"Can't we swim across?" Megan demanded.

"I'm a good swimmer," said Chris slowly, looking across towards Anglesey. "I can swim fifty lengths in thirty minutes. I'm pretty good in the sea too. But I know that if I try to swim those currents, I'll drown. Let alone someone with a seriously injured arm," he added, glancing at David.

"I don't swim well anyway." David slumped his shoulders in a gesture of defeat. "Those currents are called *braich y pwll* round here. The 'whirlpool arms'. No-one sane would try and go across."

"Well, what then?" asked Megan.

"Back into the car. We'll think," said Chris. Once inside he said, "We don't have a lot of choices. We can't go back to the village."

"Oh God, no!" Megan agreed.

"We could drive to the logging camp, but it's a dead end. We could go off on foot, but I don't fancy our chances. We can't cross here yet, but it's got to change sometime – eh, David?"

"Yes," David agreed. "It's hard to predict when. But eventually."

"Then I suggest we wait here. Facing inland so if we have to drive off we can – quickly. There's nowhere else to go, and we're safer in the car. I see you left it topped up with petrol. We should be fine to keep the engine idling for now, and the lights on, to see anyone following us. Then we wait. Eat some of those biscuits from the glove compartment. I don't know about you two but I'm starving."

"Okay. And I'll try my mobile again – just in case." Suddenly David said, "Holy shit!", making Megan jump.

"What is it?" she asked.

"A signal! A weak one, but a signal! It must be because we're so near the mainland. Except I can hardly hold it."

"Let me help." Megan held out her hand.

"Okay. 999's the quickest option."

She dialled, and got through to the Operator Assistance Centre on the second ring.

"Emergency, which service?" a man asked.

"Police please, it's extremely urgent!" Megan almost yelled.

"Police, thank you."

There was a delay then a recorded voice said, "You are in a queue, we will answer your call as soon as possible."

The seconds ticked by, each feeling like an hour as Megan gripped the phone tightly. Finally there was a click and a woman spoke. "Police Emergency, can I help you?"

"Some people are trying to kill us! Other people are dead! We're on the main road of Stawl Island near Anglesey, and can't get off it because the sandbar is flooded. We can't get away, please send help, a helicopter or something, before they find us! Please! I think it's the islanders!"

"It's okay, calm down. Can you give me your name?"

"Megan Norris."

"And you are on the road nearest Anglesey?"

"Yes, I said that!"

"Just confirming the facts. How many are there in your group?"

"Three. There's a big crowd that attacked us though."

"Is that group nearby?"

"I don't think so. We left them at the village."

"Okay, Megan. I'll pass this message on to the nearest duty officers who are free to respond. Don't worry. We have your phone number here and they may wish to get hold of you for more details, so I advise you to keep your phone turned on. I must warn you that if this is a hoax call there are severe penalties –"

"This isn't a hoax call. They tried to kill us! For God's sake, get someone out here!"

"Okay. Please close the line now and stay where you are."

There was a click.

Megan handed the phone back, and reported the emergency operator's instructions.

"You did okay," said David. He put the phone away with difficulty. It obviously hurt to move his arm. "So now we just have to wait."

Chris turned the car around, so its back was to the water. The lights shone down the road thirty feet ahead, white dashes of rain falling through the beams.

As they ate chocolate chip cookies, David thanked Chris for driving them out of the village. "You did a good job. With my arm – who knows? You handled the car like a pro."

"I've driven a Subaru before," replied Chris, always gazing out along the road, alert.

His head ached, throbs of expanding pain reaching his skull before echoing back to the centre of his brain, non-stop and almost blinding. Yet he just sat on the edge of the cast-iron bed and stared blankly ahead. The dingy bedroom's rose-patterned wallpaper surrounded him, with a mould-specked damp patch at the top of one wall where the faded paper was peeling away.

In front of him a metal and plastic object rested on the bedside table.

Every so often he would absent-mindedly itch his thigh where the rash had spread. Under his trousers recent scabs were being scratched off and bleeding afresh.

He didn't notice.

A female voice came from the object on the table. "Delta Echo Two Six, please respond."

The man slowly lifted the radio. "Two Six responding, over."

"Constable Huws, this is the control room. We've had an emergency call from the island. A woman by the name of Megan Norris saying there have been attempts on her life and requesting immediate help."

The officer scratched his leg more quickly.

"Constable Huws?" The dispatcher in the Moelfre Ward station sounded puzzled.

"I'm here. Just a bit under the weather."

As if to illustrate this, he coughed – a phlegmy, chesty sound. He didn't move the radio away from his mouth and the woman at the other end gave a sigh of distaste.

"Be aware, this could be the hoax callers you reported, but escalated to central emergency services now. At the end of the main road to Traeth Bychan, Stawl Island side. Can you attend?"

"Yes. Leave it to me. Over and out."

Constable Huws put his radio down next to David's, then cradled his head in his hands for a few seconds, baring his teeth as a drool of saliva dangled from his lower lip.

Before long he picked up the radio again.

"I think David is asleep," whispered Megan, leaning forwards. "Do you think he'll be okay?"

Chris didn't look round. "It's hard to say. He's lost a fair amount of blood. The sooner he gets to a hospital the better."

"But we can't get him to a hospital!"

"Then I can't say if he'll be okay. I'm not a doctor."

She sighed. She had hoped for *some* reassurance. "What are you then?"

"A man."

"Are you always so defensive?"

"Do you always ask so many questions?"

She slumped back, defeated. The man in the driving seat was an enigma.

He was about her age, but had a hard look to his face that suggested he had forgotten how to smile. In fact, the lack of lines on his face suggested it wasn't used to portraying any emotions at all. The short hair (shorn with clippers, she guessed) made him look like a hard man.

He was muscular too. Roughly the same height as David, but the tight short-sleeved polo shirt showed that he worked out. His hairy forearms were solid-looking. The tattoo of a seagull on his left hand, resting loosely on the steering wheel, made her think of sailors. She ruled out builder because he seemed too much in control – too guarded. So sailor or ex-military then. It would explain his efficiency of movement and alertness. Once she came to that conclusion she felt safer, and the chill in her spine receded.

The engine purred soporifically. She put the hood of her cagoule up so she wouldn't notice the wind blowing cold water through the absent rear window and closed her eyes for a few seconds.

Chris glanced back. Unbelievable. They were both asleep. Still, it was better than endless questions.

The copper was pasty. Maybe in shock.

He felt like kipping too, but wouldn't do that. Even if someone else was on watch. He didn't trust his life in anyone else's hands. No-one would value it as much as he did.

He was determined to get out of this shit no matter what.

And it really was deep shit. They had told him what happened in the woods; in turn he had described the logging camp to them (not that there was as much to tell). His mind had returned to that – it looked increasingly like something had occurred there as well.

If he'd been there earlier it might have happened to him too.

Thank God for whisky.

It was Iwan the barman who had sent him there – and according to the two in the back, Iwan was in with the murderers. Iwan may have planned it to kill him, or capture him, or whatever the fuck they wanted.

And since it was Iwan's whisky that had made him hung-over (he still felt the throb in his head – probably dehydration) then although Iwan had maybe tried to kill him, Iwan had indirectly saved his life.

Nice one, Iwan. If I run into you again I might only half-kill you.

The engine idled, though it was making a slightly different noise now. He wasn't pushing the accelerator at all. He listened carefully – no, he was wrong. It wasn't the car engine, it was something else. Another vehicle?

Into the headlights loomed a vague shape, walking quickly towards them, carrying something heavy; the engine noise was clearer ...

"Oh shit!"

He slammed the car into gear and accelerated. David and Megan both woke in a panic as the car flew forward, engine revving fully now. On impulse he aimed straight at the huge figure in a red hooded coat wielding the chainsaw. Chris planned to paint the bonnet with the bastard. Wind whipped through the car as he struggled to keep it from sliding on the wet surface, and his target seemed to expand in the harsh lights, filling the windscreen, absorbing his focus.

At the last second the man side-stepped and swung the chainsaw – Chris just glimpsed enough to see it was a huge long fucker – then sparks flew across the night with a screeching of torn metal. A side window shattered, there was a bang and the car swung to the side. It was all he could do to keep it on the road and not go into the ditch, while Megan screamed that they were all going to die, and David tried to calm her, though he looked close to disorientated panic himself.

The chainsaw must have torn through most of the side of the car. Chris knew that with kit like that the guy would make short work of the doors, and them too. For the first time the fear reared its head above the adrenalin. He faced it down.

Not now. Not yet.

“Was that a chainsaw?” asked the copper.

Ignoring him, Chris turned off the lights and slowed.

“What are you doing?” screamed Megan, who seized the rear of his seat, “Don’t stop, please, he’s back there!”

“Both of you shut up!” Chris yelled in return. “The car is fucked! We’re going nowhere fast. And unless I’m mistaken, there’s something on the road ahead between us and the village.”

Sparks were flying up behind the bared wheel-rim, grinding horribly on tarmac, but at least for now he couldn’t hear that monster of a chainsaw.

“That guy might have come from the logging camp, so we’re not going there. But if we stay on the road we’re stuck between a car or truck coming from the village, and a guy with a chainsaw from a fucking nightmare. We’re lucky we didn’t crash. Our only hope is to get away from the road, go as far as we can with the car, then move on foot.”

He wrestled the steering wheel to the left, flinging Megan into David, who grimaced with pain but didn’t scream. Maybe he wasn’t useless after all.

The car thumped off the road, heading north. He had to swing left and right to avoid the trees and boulders which were only visible at the last second. Bushes he ploughed through. At least the rear wheel and bumper weren't sparking now that they'd left the hard surface.

"Although I can't see for shit, at least by turning the lights off – crap, that was close – they won't be sure exactly where we turned off. It might confuse them. It might not, but it's the best – oh fuck, sorry – best I can think of. If you want to take over driving, be my effing guest."

Megan clung to the back of the passenger seat. "No, you're doing great," she said, with real admiration in her voice.

They were about a hundred yards from the road when the car lifted up then plunged into a ditch, smashing in the front crumple-zone and throwing them all forwards. Chris whacked into the steering wheel hard, knocking the wind out of him. He hadn't been wearing a seatbelt and gulped painfully for breath, but at least his ribcage hadn't shattered.

He flung open the door and fell out into a huge puddle with two inches of mud at the bottom; gasping, he clawed his way up the bank, only gradually regaining his breath. Rain pelted his face and eyes. The other two clambered out after him, shocked but not seriously injured.

"Turn the engine off," Chris wheezed. Megan did so, and Chris was pleased at the silence and near-darkness.

"Are you okay?" Megan asked tearfully, leaning over him.

"Yes," Chris croaked. "Though I wish the fucking airbag had gone off in my face."

It might have been a laugh or a sob or a gasp from Megan. Or all three. She helped him up.

The car or truck on the road was closer to where they had turned off.

"We'd better start running," said Chris. "Are you two okay with that?"

Megan nodded – he could just make out the movement.

"Running is what I'm good at," said David, though he looked in such a bad way that Chris resisted the urge to respond with a derogatory comment about coppers.

"I just want to ask – the huge guy you said killed someone in the woods – was he wearing a red coat?"

"Yes. You noticed too?" asked David.

"Yep. So that was probably the same guy with the chainsaw. Unless there are two psycho giants in red coats running round tonight."

They all went quiet at that thought.

None of them wanted to go through the woods in the middle of the island at night. It would be too easy to get lost, and once the pursuers found the abandoned Subaru, they would likely follow a straight line – which would take them to those woods.

They couldn't go back.

So instead they headed north-west, planning to skirt the woods and reach the cliffs. The chances of getting lost in the dark and the storm were high, but if they followed the edge of the island they would be okay.

They trudged on through marshy ground towards the coast. The terrain was both treacherous and exhausting, especially in the dark and rain. One minute they were walking swiftly over solid grass or lichen-covered rock, and the next splashing calf-deep in cold water and mud, struggling not to fall over, slopping onwards to the next bit of firm ground.

Megan spent half the time wishing she had her Land Rover still – along with the food, shelter, warmth, cross-country speed, and protection it offered. The rest of the time she just wished she could wake up in her tent and realise this was a nightmare.

When they reached the cliffs of the island's western coast they had to be careful not to venture too near the edge – the wind had picked up, and tugged and pulled at them unpredictably.

There were no lights behind, but that didn't mean they weren't being followed. Any pursuers could have turned their vehicle lights off to be more stealthy, or if they were on foot they might not be using torches. So now and again, when lightning flashed, Chris was grateful for the chance to make sure that no-one was sneaking towards them under the cover of darkness. Chris wished one of the occasional sea fogs would come in, to hide them, but suspected that the wind was too strong.

As they followed the coast north it was obvious to Chris that David was in difficulty. He had fallen twice, and Megan had helped him along a few times without David objecting. He staggered in the wind and whenever they huddled together among some bushes or low hillocks, David's eyes shut immediately, and his teeth chattered in the cold, which was sapping all of them. On top of what they had endured they were exhausted – he knew it was only adrenalin and fear that kept them moving – but to stop here on a night like this would be to risk exposure as well as being caught.

Chris had taken David's phone without David appearing to notice or care. The faint green goblin-light of the luminous display indicated no network coverage whenever he tried. He resisted the urge to smash it. They had obviously left the sweet spot with the signal, where help might look for them. It was all fucked up.

When they next stopped, squatting down out of the wind, they were parallel to Glanmor Fach woods.

"We need shelter. Warmth and rest," Chris said, arms wrapped round his body in a futile attempt to retain heat.

"Where?" asked Megan.

"Option one is the woods here."

A look of horror crossed her face. Even David, whose chin was bowed against his chest, shook his head slowly.

"No, Chris, I'm not going back there after the things that happened," Megan said. "And that man ... he might be waiting. No."

"Good, that's what I hoped you'd say. We only have one other option. The lighthouse. We can be there in less than an hour at this pace. If it's shut, we break in. And think about it – light-houses are not easy to get into, no windows, see? So if we get in, fortify it, we can stop others doing the same. We can't miss it either – even though the woods hide it from this low ground, we just follow the cliff east, past the picnic area over there. We're probably being chased, but to search every hiding hole and wood will slow the bastards down. We might just do it."

"Sh-should be empty ... not a resident lighthouse, just a maintenance stat-station," David said, teeth chattering and head bowed. "Automated on switch relays. Foghorn blasts if a pr-problem. Co-could maybe turn the lantern off or br-break it somehow, alert the Harbour Authority, get no-noticed by ships, attract help."

And maybe attract danger too, Chris thought. But he would mull the idea over for now. "Okay, we'll go there and decide what to do after we've warmed up and dried off."

"Good idea, that sounds perfect," said Megan. Then, after a pause, "I really admire you, Chris."

He was genuinely shocked. "Why?"

"Just the way you don't go to pieces. You're always thinking, having good ideas. You act quickly. You've probably saved our lives a few times already. And I know we've been slowing you down – if you left us you'd be able to get much further, hide, whatever. I'm sure you've thought of that too. So thanks."

He stared at her. Then stood and turned to look in the direction of the lighthouse. "I might need your help later. That's all."

He heard a rustling behind him, and was surprised to see Megan removing her cagoule. She helped David into it – it was like dressing a catatonic patient, Chris thought. She put the hood up and fastened it tight under David's chin. The rain was now wetting the dry fleece she'd been wearing underneath. She caught Chris looking at her as she helped David up.

"Everybody needs somebody," she said with a shrug.

Chris led the way to the lighthouse.

Lord John ap Ynyr Fychan was in his library, sipping brandy in front of the fireplace and watching a crackling fire consume dry wood and turn it to ash.

On the shelves were many books on the occult, legends, myths, the supernatural. *Lilith Magick – Authentick and Compleat, Demonolatry, Magiques de Henri-Corneille Agrippa, Malleus Maleficarum* and *De Occulta Philosophia Libri.* He had them all. Some were so old they had to be carefully handled lest they crumble. One particular prize, *De Fascino Libri Daemonum*, was bound in human skin.

He walked over to his desk and sat in the green leather chair. Putting down the brandy, he pulled over a list of names to examine it. The names of all the outsiders on the island. Next to each name were small, cryptic marks and notes in the secret shorthand he had developed. They summarised the information he had gathered by befriending the people who came here, pretending to be interested in their ghastly lives, while ferreting out details of who they were, what their families were like, and who knew they were here, so that he could assess how much they would be missed. And what cover story would serve best, if ever anything were traced to the island: "they never arrived"; "they had mentioned that they were going walking along the cliffs, even though they'd been warned of the high winds"; "they left the island early". The stories for the current visitors had been prepared along those lines, with one going missing while swimming; one whose car may have gone off the cliffs in the storm; and the new policeman perhaps drowned while rescuing someone from the sea.

Along with other preparations, such as taking the phone lines down in a way that made it look like storm damage, and temporarily sabotaging any radio communications that the islanders weren't using themselves, it would be easy to deal with the aftermath and any cover-up. The combined testimonies of the resident policeman and the Lord of the island would deal with the rest.

The list also indicated where they were to be taken from, whether or not they were to be cudgelled and sacked for later use, and their current status: dead, free or caught.

He scanned the list, and was pleased, by and large. Most of the few tourists and campers had been no problem. But there was Chris Jones. He had somehow been missed when the two itinerant loggers had been taken. And the new police officer. David Smithwick. He had gone back to his house, but had rushed out again, so the men hiding there never got a chance to cudgel and sack him.

Also the woman, Megan Norris. She should have been taken from her tent. However, the imbecile Bwystfil had ruined that when he went on his unsanctioned killing spree in the woods. Should have kept him locked in his pit until it was all over. He was proving to be as unpredictable and unruly as that deluded bitch Anne Jenkyns, or "Brân Ddu", as she ridiculously styled herself. Lord John made a mental note to create a painful way of impressing on them both who their Master was. A sinister twitch at the edge of his mouth was the only visible indication of the ideas clawing their way up from the depths of his mind.

By chance the three irritants had ended up at Yr Hen Ddyn, and the fools had put the lights on. It should have been so easy, but they got away. They had gone to the end of the road where they should have been trapped until the turn of the tide – however, despite the planning, and the radios, they had got away again.

But the hunt was on. Wherever the pests went on the island, traps had been laid. By darkness his people would creep; by darkness they would prepare. And soon the Darkness would be appeased and they would bathe in blood and carnage.

The Lighthouse

"Darkness reigns at the foot of the lighthouse." – Japanese proverb

Chris had to help support the copper for the last leg of the journey but all three of them eventually reached the lighthouse. It was about 120 feet high from the base to the top of the lamp; alternate red and white bands, each ten feet thick, ran up the sides. White walls enclosed a small compound. The gate was locked but the walls were low and Chris was over in seconds, dropping down in a crouch. Above him the lights rotated, their beams grey cones as they cut through the rain. The compound also contained a 72-tannoy fogstack, glowering alone like some huge deformed Dalek.

Moving swiftly to the only door of the lighthouse, Chris was thankful to find it unlocked. It swung inwards with a squeak. Inside was darkness. No sound, no motion. He ran back to the others. “It’s open,” he hissed, vaulting up the wall and sitting astride it. “Let’s get you two over.”

It was a struggle getting the copper up, but Megan climbed over the wall with an agility that surprised Chris. He lowered David down; David did his best to help and not make too much noise, but involuntary groans of pain came from him as he was manhandled. Chris dropped down again and the three moved over to the door.

“Urgh!” exclaimed Megan in horror as something crunched underfoot. “What’s that?”

Chris glanced down. “Dead birds. Maybe attracted to the light at night,” he guessed. “Probably get stunned or break their necks. Looks like no-one has cleared up for a while.”

“Poor things,” whispered Megan, skirting the piles of little bodies.

Chris turned his attention back to the lighthouse interior. It was pitch black, but, in a second stroke of luck, a lightning flash gave him a brief glimpse of the layout. Some barrels and cans stacked up, boxes, and, about twenty feet away to his left, the start of the wrought-iron staircase running around the interior circumference of the building. After the thunder finished rumbling Chris listened – but there were still no sounds of movement within the lighthouse.

And there was no point putting it off.

The three moved inside and closed the door. Chris felt along the wall and found a light switch. The fluorescents flickered then buzzed into life. He checked the wooden door. No bolts. There was a keyhole but no visible key to lock it with.

He dragged the heaviest crates and furniture over to the door, piling them up. After sitting David in a chair, Megan helped as best she could, until there was quite a sturdy barrier on the inside.

"That should hold a few people for a while," Chris said with more confidence than he felt.

Lord John was in the cellar of *Plas Dof*. His mansion; his home; his feudal castle ...

His laboratory.

He never allowed anyone into this part of the house.

He *forced* a few people; and generally that was not problematic, as the people he brought here wouldn't give away his secrets to the locals or anyone else.

Because they ended up dead.

The bare bulb in the ceiling was draped with old cobwebs, thickened with dust. He glanced round at the dirt elsewhere – on the wine rack, the tool shelves, the floor. It was a shame he couldn't allow the cleaners down here.

Just in case.

Ignoring the arched doorways leading to the laundry room and workshop, he took a large torch from a shelf at the bottom of the stone steps and pushed open the door to the coal room. He hardly used coal for heating any more, but nonetheless the room was filled to the ceiling in one corner, below the coal chute.

The torch flicked on and the beam was swept around the room, occasionally glinting off the small shiny patches that showed amongst the dusty black coal. All was in order.

His feet shuffled grittily over to the opposite corner, and he pulled at a brick. It swung on a hinge revealing a small keyhole. He took a polished key from the pocket of his jacket and turned it in the lock, before dropping the key back into his pocket and patting it like a good dog.

A section of wall swung away from him when he pushed, revealing a short corridor. He entered and closed the wall behind. A switch brought on a ceiling-mounted nightlight just bright enough to see his way by.

He ignored his supply room, which had enough food and water to last over six months, as well as a coal-fired electricity generator. Just in case. Instead he entered the second of three doors, only sparing a swift glance towards the barred steel one at the end of the corridor.

Fluorescent bulbs flicked on one by one as the door opened, illuminating a large room full of laboratory equipment: drug and chemical cabinets; a stainless steel autopsy table to which he had secured leather retaining straps; a large sink; a computer and microscope; a centrifuge; a white distillation chiller; and a hydrogen peroxide vapour bio-decontamination device. One unit supported a monitor with an ancient VHS recorder underneath, but it was currently switched off. He picked up a clipboard and pen – the inventory of the most recent tests, drugs used, results. He scanned the list and tutted.

Taking the clipboard with him, he went back to the corridor and the barred steel door. He removed the heavy bar from two hooks. The handle of the door was cold as he pulled it open and entered to a smell of ammonia.

A click and the fluorescents blinked and buzzed into life, revealing various-sized cages. A few of the smaller ones were occupied, but the animals in them were silent, watching him through the bars or lying still at the back. There were just a few rodents now, mostly unused. It was a chore cleaning out animals, removing the dead and those that had been gnawed by others due to confinement stress. Of course, it was a thrill to find one with a paw torn away, or young with their heads bitten off by their mothers – but there were more interesting subjects these days than guinea pigs and rats.

It was the man in the large, old sheep cage that got his attention, the man with the slack face like a bubbled wax mask on the verge of melting. The man's bloodshot eyes tried unsuccessfully to focus on Lord John, before the misshapen head flopped forward again, and a mucoid gurgle came from his throat.

A definite failure, Lord John thought.

He took a hypodermic syringe from the tray outside the man's cage, and filled it with something new he had concocted, eager to observe the effects and record more data. He tried to control his excited breathing, and ignore the swelling in his trousers.

While he was the Turner on the island, nothing could go wrong.

This room seemed to be just for storage: crates, boxes, large tins of lubricating oil, a few empty barrels of fuel, tables, lobster pots, some fishing nets. The room was around thirty-five feet in diameter, the full size of the lighthouse inside. As Chris had expected, there were no windows. Light from inside couldn't leak out to give them away. Metal lattice stairs ran up the inside of the grey walls to a closed trapdoor in the cathedral-like vaulted ceiling, about forty feet above. No-one had come down, or made any noise upstairs, but that didn't mean there was no-one there.

David was shivering all the time now. Megan put her hand to his forehead.

"Hot," she mouthed silently over David's head.

"Fever," suggested Chris. "Loss of blood, exhaustion, very possibly an infection too. I'd best check out the rest of the lighthouse now, make sure it's safe. You wait with him. If anything happens, shout me – otherwise I'll be back as soon as I can."

Megan nodded.

"You're doing okay," Chris told her, snapping a loose bit of wood about two feet long from the edge of a crate. Then he searched among the smelly fishing nets until he found a bundle that was small enough to be useful. He put it over his shoulder and ascended, wood held in his left hand. His footsteps clanked on the metal grilles. When he reached the trapdoor he peered down.

The other two looked remarkably small. Megan was watching him. He made an okay sign with his thumb raised, and she copied him.

Putting the tip of the wood against the trapdoor, he pushed up, so that, as the gap widened, if anyone were waiting there with a gun or blade, it would be his stick that got splintered, not his head.

The trapdoor opened without incident. He dared to peep through the gap.

There was no-one standing there waiting to kill him.

However, there was a light switch on the wall a few feet away. Pushing the trapdoor up and up, it reached the point of balance. Another nudge and it whistled back, slamming into the floor with a crash that echoed dully round the chamber.

He edged around the wall, using the pale light from below as a guide. The switch clicked. Lights flickered. Again, a single large room with a high vaulted ceiling, and stairs running up to another closed trapdoor. The walls in this room were whitewashed. It looked like a kitchen. No windows – but kitchen units, cooker, big fridge and freezer, table and chairs.

He descended. "Megan, it's a kitchen on the floor above. It looks like a lighthouse that can be lived in. So there should be food and towels, maybe a first aid kit. I'll carry David up."

"What about the door here?"

"We'll hear if anyone tries to come in."

It was hard work getting David up the stairs. Chris hooked his arms under David's armpits, Megan under his knees. David groaned occasionally, but didn't say anything rational. At one point Chris thought he heard a noise from somewhere, a vague scratching sound: but when they stopped moving there was nothing. Just the creaks of a tower in the wind.

They sat David in a chair, then dried themselves off with some towels, Megan washing the remains of blood from her hands first. She rummaged for supplies, and soon had a kettle boiling. She also found a first aid kit, but it only contained plasters and a few aspirin two years out of date. She kept them to the side anyway, and prepared three cups of sweet coffee. The milk in the fridge was sour, but steaming black coffee would still be heaven.

Chris found a hefty, long-bladed chopping knife in a drawer and tucked it into his belt. In one of the cupboards was an unlabelled brown bottle with some liquid in. He unstoppered it and sniffed – whisky. Most of the food in the fridge didn't look very edible, but in the freezer was a sliced loaf. It was a month past its date but should be okay. There was a toaster on one unit, so he did a plate of dry toast. They took everything to the table.

"Quite a feast, eh?" he joked, stomach grumbling furiously.

The smell of the strong coffee even brought David round. He still shivered but his eyes were open.

Megan helped David to take a few painkillers – his hand was too shaky to hold the glass of water. He nodded at her gratefully after swallowing them.

Chris took the bottle he'd found and added a dash of the contents to his coffee.

"What's that?" asked Megan.

"Whisky. Medicinal. It'll warm up my centre. Want some?"

"Okay," she replied. "Though normally I hate the stuff."

"Me too," croaked David, startling them.

Chris laughed as he poured it into their coffees. "Glad you're still with us," he said to David, who just nodded.

David refused toast but – again, with Megan's help – drank some of the coffee, then slumped, eyes closed. Megan and Chris ate – dry toast had never tasted so good – and sipped their own drinks. The cups were warming between their hands, the aroma rose on the steam and smelt like normal life, and the hot liquid with whisky warmed the frozen blocks of ice inside their bodies.

They didn't talk. Just stared into the almost-black circles in their cups, watching the darkness disappear until they were finally empty, savouring the peace.

Chris eventually broke the silence. "I'm going to look round the next floor, see if there's anything useful. If all the rooms are the same height then it might be the last floor. You wait here with David."

"Okay. I was thinking I could use hot water, towels, clean his arm up a bit."

Chris looked at the semi-conscious David, doubtful that it would make any difference. "Good idea. You're quite plucky, you know that?"

She laughed. "I don't feel it." Then, with a more serious tone, "But the one thing I'm really glad of is that I'm not alone."

Chris nodded and squeezed her shoulder.

While Megan got on with removing the cagoule from David, Chris headed up the steps with the heavy knife and net. He used a hand this time to lift the second trapdoor and again saw a light switch. It looked safe, so after lowering the trapdoor open he flicked the switch.

The lights came on revealing another white-washed room. Two fluorescent tubes flickered annoyingly. This room had a bed, wardrobes and other furniture on one side, and a desk, CB radio set and electric fire on the other. All clear.

For peace of mind he clanked up the stairs around this room too. There was rumbling from the floor above. As carefully as before, he made his way into this upper room, where the noise grinding in the darkness was louder, some kind of machinery.

When the light came on he could see a large-cogged oily engine running, turning a metal rod which ran up through a hole in the low ceiling; probably rotating the lantern, he thought. Around the edge of the room was a small workshop and what was obviously control gear for the lighthouse, even though the mechanisms mystified Chris.

A quick scan around confirmed this room was empty of danger too. He ascended stairs once more, wondering how tall the damn tower was.

The trapdoor this time had two bolts on the underside – the only one to have them. He pushed it up a few inches and was assailed by howling wind carrying a gust of cold rain into his face from the darkness outside. It was the top of the tower.

He lowered the trapdoor and bolted it closed, before going down to Megan.

"There isn't much more I can do," she whispered, gesturing at David, who had the sleeve of his tracksuit rolled up, and a clean towel tightly fastened round his forearm with string. Dark spots had soaked through the towel. "He's still bleeding, but less. He didn't even murmur while I did it. I'm really worried about him."

"There's a bed and a heater on the next floor. Let's take him up there. He'll be more comfortable and warmer. When he comes round we could try and get him to drink some water, raise his liquid levels."

They struggled to carry his dead weight up one more flight and lay him on the bed. He looked a mess with dark red patches all over his tracksuit top. Megan pulled the fire as close as the flex would allow and turned it on full. The elements glowed orange and began to give out heat.

Chris went over to the radio communications set on a table by the writing desk and examined the mess of wires and dials, then powered it up. After an irritatingly long wait it finally crackled into life, but there was just static. He couldn't pick up any signals. He wasn't sure if it was damaged or if he was using it wrongly. He kept turning the dial anyway, and occasionally pressed the button on the microphone, and said: "If anyone can hear this, please help. There are a group of murderers on Ynys Diawl, and people are dead. Three of us are still alive, but one is in very urgent need of medical attention. We are in the lighthouse near the north of the island. We desperately need help."

Megan stood next to him. "Do you think anyone will hear?"

"I don't know. Probably not. Even if they did they might think it was a joke. It's all we can do though."

A noise. Like a child giggling.

Chris snatched up the knife and looked around the room. There was no-one. Megan stepped half-behind him, a hand on his upper arm.

Again giggling. At first Chris though it was David, and felt a shiver of apprehension. As he began to move, though, the wardrobe next to the bed opened and a man in a yellow sou'wester and wellies, with staring, wide eyes stepped out. In one hand he had a cruel, curved fishing knife. Chris moved as quickly as he could, but before he reached the bed the man looked down at David, grinned, and put the point of the blade against his throat. With a swift movement he cut through David's windpipe and at least part of an artery. Blood spurted over the pillows and David's face. David gasped and sucked for bubbling air, twitching but hopefully not conscious, and then the man just stood there, knife slackly at his side, giggling at David's jerky body movements as the sheets soaked up blood around him.

Megan screamed and covered her eyes while Chris unslung the net and held it out in his right hand, posture lowered, large knife at the ready in his left, and advanced cautiously towards the madman, the bastard madman who had been hidden there, listening all along.

David arched his back then stopped convulsing.

The killer watched Chris approach, his soulless eyes weeping thick liquid.

Chris flung the net. The man put his arms out and was partially tangled. Chris ran forward to stab him, but the man shifted and grabbed Chris's knife arm. His grip was strong and he kept Chris's arm lowered.

With a gasp Chris realised he had been stabbed in the upper leg with the vicious curved knife, not too deeply into the muscle, but deeply enough to hurt and bleed a lot. He elbowed the man in the face, snapping his head back, then moved behind him, wrapping his right arm around the man's neck and trying to choke him. In the struggle they both fell, smashing into the open wardrobe door so that the wood split and it hung by one hinge only, then they fell to the floor. As they did so the madman smashed Chris's hand against the floor twice and his knife skittered across the floorboards. The killer clambered on top of him, the net now tangling them both, and thrust the curved knife at Chris's face. Chris used both his hands to keep the man away, but he was deceptively strong, almost unbelievably so for someone his size.

Chris struggled to get a knee free to strike with, or to deflect the inexorable progress of the knife, but couldn't get enough movement. He struggled to wriggle away but the man was pressing closer, actually drooling and giggling, and when Chris's foot slipped in his own blood and as he collapsed back under the knife, he realised he was running out options.

The man suddenly tensed, back arched, and Chris took this split-second opportunity to move away from the curved knife so it just missed his face. He headbutted the man, making a wet snapping noise, then threw his weight to one side. The man rolled onto his back, and again tried to slash Chris with the knife, but Chris used his left arm to block, sat astride him and punched him in the face hard with two quick right jabs. The man's grip on the curved knife loosened. Chris grabbed it out of his hand then, still sat astride his abdomen, stabbed the man in the chest again and again using both hands.

"You fucking bastard! Die you fucking bastard!"

He stabbed until the man stopped squirming, until he hadn't gasped for some time, until Chris's hands were covered in blood and part of the knife had snapped off inside the man's ribs. The man's chest bubbled blood and air and the yellow raincoat was ripped to red shreds around his chest.

Only then did Chris drop the broken knife, which splattered into the growing pool of blood

The room stank. David was dead on blood-soaked sheets; the man was a bloody ruin; red streaks were splashed on the wall, the furniture, the wardrobe; Chris's face, body and clothes were smeared. When he stood up his lower legs were dripping red from the pool he had been kneeling in.

Megan was standing nearby, pale, holding Chris's knife in both hands. There was blood on that too.

"I stabbed him," she said hoarsely. "I stabbed him. I've never stabbed anyone before. And then you killed him."

"I killed him." He stepped towards her, careful not to slip in the blood. She still gazed at where he had been.

"He was killing you. He would have killed you. I had to stab him, didn't I?"

"You did."

He reached out and took the knife gently from her fingers. She didn't resist.

"I stabbed him."

"You had to. You saved my life."

He put the knife on a table.

"And David's dead, isn't he?"

"David's dead."

She cried, huge sobs, her whole body shaking, and although he was covered in blood he hugged her for a long time, comforting her, while his own eyes just stared ahead.

Lord John replaced the square black microphone and stared at the radio transceiver with a look of concern. He had tried to contact Meurig and Emyr, but either they weren't answering or there was something wrong with their radios. All he could pick up were crackles and what sounded like grunting.

Perhaps he had been too eager, and the formula used on the men during the earlier ceremony was too strong, too chaotic.

That would help to create the right conditions for madness and killing, but was not so good if one wanted regular and coherent reports.

He didn't like not knowing what was happening. This was to be the greatest night of his life, planned in minute detail for many years, with patience so vast that he admired his own abilities.

The end was so close now. All the calculations said so. Tonight was a night of power far in excess of Walpurgisnacht. All forces converged on this time; all prophecies hinted at it; all stars were aligned. Years of observing the flows, tides and weather systems had paid off: he was the only person capable of predicting the effects of the currents between Stawl Island and Anglesey. Science had confirmed what the deep space stars had suggested. He had predicted this night would be accompanied by a huge storm, and he had been proved correct, he thought smugly. The storm had come, the island made inaccessible – a whole world unto itself, with him the ruler – and it all proved beyond any doubt in his mind that he was correct.

It was as if, by being the last of his line, all the power of his ancestors had culminated in him, the sediments gathering and sinking into the lower blood of which he had grown. He was the fruit of their blood, and had built on their work and improved it a hundredfold. He wasn't fully sure *how* it would happen – but every sign pointed to the incontrovertible fact that tonight there would be a reversal, a huge change in the power of the island, and he would help to nurture then harvest it.

Him. Him.

His ancestors had failed partly for circumstances they couldn't help, because of the primitive tools at their disposal.

Some had failed because they were too weak. These were the strain he thought of as the Do Gooders. They were too soft on people. They had pandered to the Welsh: speaking their ugly language and changing their name from noble Weston to Ynyr Fychan. His ancestors were English first, and had come as rulers. The Do Gooders seemed to have forgotten that, somewhere along the line. However, Lord John's rediscovery of Turning had reversed that mistake, and he had controlled and changed and moulded minds as clay; worked on the islanders' natural enmities and fears, indoctrinating them to hate outsiders and see them only as potential victims and sources of income and revenge – an outlet and direction for the frustrated hate bred into them.

The other strain in his family was what he called the Realists. They would pursue any avenue that looked promising. He saw himself belonging to that camp. However, the weakness of this side of his ancestors was a propensity for madness. So many of them had succumbed to the family trait. Suicides, paranoia, seeing things that weren't there, strange fantasies – maybe even changing to a Welsh surname were all symptoms.

But he, Lord John, was pure; the only fully sane member of his family (and, by a nice coincidence, the only living one). He had broken the curse of blood-madness by following Great Uncle Philip's ideas and perfecting them; combined with his devotion to the Dark Ones in exchange for power.

And so the negative energy had grown, and the ceremonies and sacrifices had led to tonight as surely as the path of a man falling into a spike-filled pit led to the bottom, and impalement on the point of fate.

Tonight was all or nothing; the night to offer souls on the wind, and to sow fear, and pain, and madness – and the change he would experience, the change he had been promised, was close.

Chris sat her down. She was pliant.

He pulled the edges of the sheets up so they covered David's body. He was now just a few pillows under a red sheet, that's all.

He checked the other wardrobe, knife ready. Empty. Chris took the two folded green blankets from the bottom then limped back to the bed.

One he spread over the bed. Over the pillows and red sheets. One over the killer. The blood soaked through immediately, but it was an improvement.

Megan sat in the chair where he had put her, in silence. The chair faced away from the bed. He would leave her until she was ready.

He looked again in the wardrobe where he had found the blankets. He removed a dark green wool turtleneck jumper, a paint-stained shirt obviously worn for decorating, and some canvas trousers. He took off his own jeans. The cut wasn't too deep. He found a spare pillowcase in the wardrobe and used his knife to cut it and tear it into strips. He tied them around his leg as tight as he could, over a small bandage made with a thicker strip. He put the canvas trousers on. They were loose but he used the belt from his jeans and they stayed up then.

He was about to ask Megan if she would be okay on her own for a few minutes – just while he went down to the kitchen to clean his face and arms of blood before finishing getting dressed – when he heard a banging noise. It was coming from downstairs. The lighthouse entrance.

Megan looked up at him.

"It could be help," Chris said quietly.

But their eyes gave away what they both really felt.

Arrivals And Departures

"O miserable man, what a deformed monster has sin made you! God made you 'little lower than the angels'; sin has made you little better than the devils." – Joseph Alleine, *An Alarm To The Unconverted*

Chris dressed quickly in the shirt and jumper, wiping his face on the sleeves of the polo shirt he was discarding. It would have to do.

He rushed down the stairs with Megan, the kitchen knife back in his hand, but when they reached the ground floor they were certain it wasn't help that had arrived. There was the sound of splintering wood as sharp implements hacked at the door.

"It'll hold for a while. Come on, let's make it harder for them."

As they heaved furniture and sizable boxes in front of the door, Megan asked, "How did they find us?"

He grunted and threw a crate on top of the pile. They wouldn't be able to open the door with all that inside. They would have to break their way through. "Could have been when I tried the radio. Maybe they just came here anyway, looking for us. It was an obvious place to go. Right, that will hold them for a bit. Wait here, I'll be back soon. If anything happens, come up yelling."

"Where are you going?" she pleaded, her shrill voice competing with the splintering wood and bangs at the door.

"To check out what we're up against."

He pressed the handle of the knife into her hands and ran up the stairs, ignoring the pain and stiffness in his leg.

In the kitchen he took a handful of painkillers and a swig of whisky, grabbed another knife, and carried on up to the final trapdoor. He unbolted it, threw it open, and climbed up into the maelstrom.

Wind screamed at him, buffeting him about and lashing him with rain. A narrow metal walkway ran around the glass windows behind which the lantern and bullseye lenses rotated, blinding when beaming his way. The lighthouse mechanism had a domed roof which didn't extend over the walkway to offer any protection from the elements. A steel ladder led up to it. Around the outside of the walkway was a metal railing, four feet high.

Head down against the wind, and leaning against the glass, Chris made his way around the walkway's grating. The island stretched away to the south, a dark mass hardly separable from the crashing sea in the darkness.

He leaned over the railing, clinging tight, and saw the group of people trying to get in a hundred feet below. Some carried powerful torches, others weapons. It was definitely the villagers. One of them looked up, saw Chris silhouetted by the powerful lights behind him, and pointed – then let out an unearthly scream that seemed to stretch on and on, grating as fingernails on a blackboard.

Further away, the lights of other torches were making their way towards the lighthouse.

Something had warned them but there was no point worrying about it. It was the same truth he had faced since the hard knocks of his too-short childhood: his luck always ran out in the end.

"Fuckers!" Chris yelled. In anger he threw the knife down amongst the group, but couldn't make out what damage he did. He wished he had David's gun now, wherever he'd got it from.

He spotted a bulky item attached to the railing. It was marked "Escape Apparatus"; an emergency ladder, which when released dropped in ten-foot sections down to the base of the lighthouse. Or it would have, if someone hadn't removed the handle next to the yellow arrow saying "Pull release lever". The arrow now pointed to a twisted stump where the lever had been sheared off.

He sprinted back down to Megan, who was watching the door being hacked apart, flinching with each rending noise.

"I went to the top," he told her.

"Lots of people?"

He nodded. "Too many to fight."

"Why don't we go up, try and block the trapdoors?" Megan suggested eagerly. "It will take them time to get through. Maybe they'll give up."

Chris didn't think they would give up, but told her it was a good idea. And after that they could gather things to throw off the lighthouse, maybe kill or injure some of them.

He knew it was always better to do *something*. It would prevent fear from paralysing them.

They made their way up to the kitchen level, and dragged anything moveable over to the trapdoor, piling it on top. Even drawers and pans, it all added up to a large mound that would take time to get through, and hinder the pursuers on the stairs after that.

Meurig Evans arrived back at the hunting lodge, swaying drunkenly, his feet betraying him. It was hard to open his eyes because of the sticky gum forming there. He staggered up the steps then thudded into the door, a hacking cough leaving drops of blood on some rabbit skin fixed there. He tried to rub it away with a shaking hand but it just smeared and looked like more than it was.

He entered the hut and, after slamming the door behind him, he sank to his knees and clutched his throat, struggling to breathe. He was still alive – the throbbing pain in his skull told him that – but weak. Every movement made him wince.

He leaned back against the wall. If only he was more like the beast! A creature that feels no ordinary physical pain, that fears nothing but the punishments of himself and Lord John. A creature that exists only to hunt, to kill, to torture. To pass the pain that had been its only experience in life on to others.

Even animals sensed its ferocious and implacable nature; Meurig had often witnessed the woods go silent when it was around. *Duw*, how he admired it. A monument to Lord John's skill.

Yet Meurig's own body was collapsing around him. Why? It was something to do with the last communion drink, he was sure; but for the Lord to harm him? Or for his plans to fail? It was unthinkable.

Well, that's the end of it. Not for him to worry over.

Another coughing fit, and this time he could taste the metallic tang in his mouth. He spat on the floor, a crimson foamy gob. A string of red saliva hung from his chin. With each cough the agony in his head got worse, blocking out everything else.

He thought he sensed a familiar shape in the shadows by the far corner beside a mounted deer skull, a reddish hulk that seemed to retract slightly when he focussed his gaze on it.

"*Y Crymanwr, ie? Wedi dod amdana i o'r diwedd?*" ["Reaper, yeah? Come for me at last?"]

No response.

"*Bwystfil. Ti sy'na*," he croaked. "*Tyd!*" ["Beast. It's you. Come!"]

Still no sound from the shadows. Unused to disobedience, Meurig glared at the blurred outlines with one eye, and he spoke the Conditioning Words, the words that must be obeyed, words drilled into the Bwystfil's head since it was old enough to learn – the Lord's words. Then he gave his final command.

"*Lladda fi rŵan, Bwystfil. Dw i'n siŵr dy fod di wedi bod eisiau drwy dy –*" hacking, choking, it took a while to get his breath back, "*– trwy dy oes ofnadwy. Rŵan. Dw i'n gofyn i ti wneud.*"

["Kill me now, Beast. I'm sure you have wanted to all your – all your dreadful life. Now. I'm asking you to do it."]

Meurig expected a huge man in a red hooded coat to take a few tentative steps forward. He expected a distorted face hinted at by the shapes seen in the shadows of the hood. He expected a shambling ogre, but one that sometimes whined like a terrified dog; something with a manner more like a child expecting punishment than a beast. Maybe a roar this time as the fiend grabbed Meurig's head in both hands, and twisted; he pictured a welcome cracking of bone and for the agony of breathing to end.

Nothing.

Meurig crawled forwards, dragging his body, to confirm what his blurred vision showed.

But the creature he had known all its life, that he had helped the Lord create, was not there. It was just a shadow in the shape of a CB radio on a heavy table; beyond was a fresh skin stretched across a rack.

The beast wasn't there.

And he was so weary.

With a sob he crawled to the trapdoor, used his remaining energy to lift it, then pulled his body down into the blackness of the cellar, letting the trap slam shut behind him.

Once the creaking stairs below the floor ceased their protest, the lodge was silent.

Chris was putting the last few heavy jars onto the pile, slotting them into gaps, when he heard a muffled revving noise from downstairs; a noise with a changing pitch, accompanied by cracking and snapping sounds. He had already heard it once tonight.

He put his forehead against the cold wall, closed his eyes tight, and clenched his fists.

"What is it, Chris?"

She hadn't recognised the sound. Good. There might be hope yet if she didn't panic.

"Nothing, come on upstairs now, we'll do the same there."

He grabbed her hand and pulled her up to the next floor, getting her away from that buzzing noise that made him think of doors and furniture being carved apart like butter.

They shoved furniture over the trapdoor in the bedroom. Blood seeped through his trousers, wet on his thigh. Then Chris made Megan turn away. He dragged the bed which still held David's body, then the killer's corpse, leaving blood smeared across the floor. Blood everywhere, and more to come, but the extra weight on the trapdoor bought them time. Maybe only minutes, thanks to the new arrival downstairs, but Chris took whatever he could get. He was sweating, aching, scared – and could now hear debris being kicked aside on the ground level.

They were in. Next they'd be cutting their way into the kitchen.

Megan spun round, eyes wide, hand over her mouth in horror. This time she *had* recognised what the revving noise meant.

He nodded, grabbed her hand and yanked to get her moving, dragging her up to the mechanism floor. He saw how pale she was: a walking corpse.

Then blind fury broke out, as if a pin had been pulled from a grenade inside him. "Those fucking bastards! I can't deal with shit-hole twats like that!"

He grabbed a wrench, strode over to the rotating engine, scanned it, then thrust the wrench between two cogs. There was a tremendous grinding vibration throughout the whole floor; with a squeal and a judder the mechanism stopped, and the light ceased its turning.

"I didn't want to do that before in case it gave us away, added to all my other fuck ups. No harm now. I don't expect the cunting cavalry, but what the hell."

"It's not your fault, Chris."

"Thanks."

There wasn't much to drag over the trapdoor here. They did what they could. Then they rushed up to the roof, and the shock of wind and rain took Chris's breath away. He looked over the edge, mind racing, every option a dead end. Then he gestured back down.

Once out of the storm he said, "There isn't any point throwing things over. Most of them are inside now. Others are still arriving." He made a conscious effort to ignore the persistent revving of the chainsaw as it sawed through obstacles into the bedroom.

"What about making a rope of some kind, from sheets or something?"

He shook his head while rain pelted through the open trapdoor. "Even if it reached to the ground and held, the people down there would see us. Some were shining torches towards the top of the lighthouse. And to be honest, even with time – which we haven't got, Megan – there's not enough in this room or the one below to make anything useful. And we can't get to the rope on the ground floor now. Fuck! There's an emergency ladder at the top, that might have been a better option, but someone – someone I would love to spend five minutes alone with – has sabotaged it. Maybe with time I could fix it, but there is no time."

There was crashing on the floor below, cutting, engine revving, footsteps clattering up the steps to the last blocked trapdoor. It began to vibrate as it was pounded with fists or weapons, rattling the items on top. The chainsaw's volume increased as its wielder approached the final obstacle to take over the task. They'd soon be in the machine room, then the roof. Two minutes, tops.

"Can we hide?" she asked. "In this room, or hang over the edge of the lighthouse, hope they don't see us and give up, go away, or …"

Tears swam in her eyes. Chris hated to take away her hope. But he had to. "They'd find us. And do us in, screaming. I won't go down like that. Come on."

He led her to the top of the lighthouse again, and closed the last trapdoor. If only there were bolts on the upper side, or something up here to block it with, to buy a few more minutes.

The storm assaulted them, but he held her shoulders firmly and looked into her eyes. He had to shout to be heard, but it was better than the roaring of the chainsaw cutting into the room below, stealing all thought and sanity and hope.

There had to be hope.

"We aren't helpless!" he yelled at her. "We can still survive, get away."

"How?" Megan shouted back, wanting to believe.

He moved her to the edge, pointed down, hoped there was enough time to persuade her. She followed the direction of his arm with her eyes. They were on the north-east edge of the lighthouse, out of sight of the entrance. It was the point nearest the cliffs. A hundred feet below, the grass ended. Then the cliff descended to the crashing sea beneath, just beyond the white wall.

Worry and puzzlement showed on her face equally, as if she refused to understand him, didn't dare contemplate what he was suggesting. He looked steadily into her eyes until she shook her head in horror. "My God, that's crazy, we'll die, falling that far, over a cliff! Into the sea! There are rocks and currents and –"

"Listen! The currents are weaker here; it's the other side of the island, in the channel, where they are strongest. Think how high the water is now – it's high tide, the rocks are deep below the surface. People have survived falls out of aeroplanes when their parachutes haven't opened. I've read that, so this is nothing for two fit people like you and me. We hit the water, swim south, get to the beach, hide there. They'll assume we're dead!" He was making it up on the spot, speaking quickly to hide flaws (from both of them) as well as to save time, but there was almost no time left to talk.

"But the distance to the cliff edge ..."

"It's our only option!" he yelled. "The base of the lighthouse isn't far from the edge of the cliff here. The wind's blowing out to sea like a mother-fucking hurricane, we felt it just then. If we go to the very top it will catch us, take us further out, just for a few extra feet. Don't be scared, Megan. We can clear it. We really can!"

In his heart he suspected this was suicide, but it was better than the alternative. Much as he wanted to hide, much as he wanted to hope it was all somehow a mistake, he knew they were dead either way.

Better on their own terms.

"I believe you," she said so quietly he only understood by watching her lips.

He climbed the narrow ladder to the top of the domed metal roof then helped her up. The wind was blasting ferociously here, and they crawled to the centre where a man-height lightning rod pointed up at the sky. Only when holding on to this did he feel secure enough to stand.

First he took off the green jumper that would only soak up water, and threw it, watching the wind snatch it and whiz it out to the east, over the edge of the lighthouse and down out of sight.

"See! I said the wind was blowing our way," he yelled with a forced smile.

They both stood now, clutching the lightning rod.

"If you hold my hand then I promise you'll be okay. We'll run and jump –"

"It's been nice knowing you, Chris Jones," she interrupted, looking at him as if he was something better than he was.

Shit.

If he was going to die, maybe one less lie might help his case afterwards. And there was no point keeping it to himself.

"Turner. My real name is Chris Turner!" he shouted, mouth near her ear. "I lied to you and the policeman. I'm a criminal. An armed robber. Or was, until I came here."

"What the hell does it matter now?" yelled Megan. "I thought you were a sailor."

"You're a brave girl, Megan Norris. Are you ready to go?"

"No! But I once read a book called *Feel The Fear And Do It Anyway*. I can feel the fear."

Rain ran down her face. Chris suspected it hid tears.

At the edge of his vision he saw a huge red-hooded figure coming over the top of the ladder behind them; he was sure he could hear the chainsaw chugging, then it was lifted into sight as the man got ready to crawl after them. Chris was glad Megan was looking at him, and hadn't seen.

There were no choices left. If it had just been a single person with a knife – or even two people – he would have fought. But not someone with a chainsaw, backed up by an army of psychos.

On an impulse he kissed his seagull tattoo, then grabbed Megan's hand, squeezed it tightly, and pulled her to the edge at a run.

It should have worked, but things happened too fast – the curved blade of a long-handled scythe swished through the air just above the end of the roof, a blind swing from someone on the walkway below, but it was enough for Megan to pull back, yanking Chris with her. He lost his footing on the wet metal and fell on his backside, sliding towards the edge. He just managed to dig his heels in and struggle back as the scythe blade swung again and clanged onto the roof where his shins had been a second before. He had lost Megan's grip, and when he spun round she was scrabbling on her hands and knees, soaking hair in her eyes blinding her, heading towards the man in the red hooded coat.

"Megan! Turn round!"

She wiped the hair out of her eyes and saw her danger. The huge guy stood with the chainsaw held out, taking tentative steps forwards. The roar of it was terrifying, and seemed to drown out the noise of wind and drumming rain. The man was having trouble standing upright; the gale whipped at him and his red coat and caught the long blade of the chainsaw, making him slip about. His upper body seemed much bulkier than his legs, Chris noted.

"Come here!" he yelled to Megan.

She scrabbled over, but the man in red took quick strides and suddenly he was between Megan and Chris. Megan screamed and crawled backwards, away from Chris.

The man in red slipped again, and the whirring edge of the chainsaw narrowly missed his foot. He seemed to realise it was too dangerous to wield on that surface, in that blasting wind, and lay it down near the edge, the engine now dead.

Chris knew he could still jump – but if he did it would mean leaving Megan behind. There was no way she could circle past the big man to get to the side they needed to jump from.

The man in red reached into his coat and removed a large and wicked-looking hunting knife, turning from Megan to Chris and back again. He took two steps towards Megan. There was no more time for thinking.

"Oi, you big fucker!" Chris yelled. "Pick on someone your own size!"

Chris had no idea what he was going to do. Take it second by second. Plans weren't worth shit anyway. He stood, but the wind buffeted him dangerously, so he got into a low crouch which felt safer, even though the wound in his upper leg ached more in that position.

The big man turned to face him. It was obvious that there was a deformity, maybe a hunch, barely hidden by the coat; the head was wrong too, misshapen under that tightly-fastened hood. Although he couldn't see clearly, Chris got the feeling that Red Hood was grinning.

Another man in a checked shirt was on the roof now, and crawling towards Megan. There wasn't much time.

A strong gust of wind rocked the top of the lighthouse. The man in red almost fell as it slammed into his bulk, and Chris's shoe slipped. He couldn't get a grip. He needed an advantage. He knelt and pulled off his shoes and socks as quickly as he could – socks thrown to the wind, a shoe held in each hand. The metal roof was icy cold on his feet, but by digging his toes in he felt slightly more purchase.

While Chris did this Red Hood had been edging cautiously towards him, down the convex roof. He was almost upon Chris as he finally stood. The man swung the knife out in vicious swipes at face height, forcing Chris back to the edge, trying to keep a low balance. He threw a shoe as hard as he could at his opponent's face, just as the swinging arm went past, a good connecting throw that didn't hurt but surprised the big man and made him flinch back a step or two, almost falling in the process.

He was top-heavy, uncoordinated; he had a weakness. Chris had to use it against him. He would only have one chance to turn the situation round. He had to unbalance him further.

Megan was still free but Chris saw that someone had reached over the roof's edge and grabbed her ankle. She was struggling and kicking, but Chris couldn't think about that; Red Hood would need all his focus.

"You big fucking freak! You big pussy, scared of me, eh? Come and get some if you're not scared, you bastard, I'll rip your fucking head off, I eat ugly bastards for breakfast; that's it, I bet you're hiding your face because you're such an ugly fuck you would make me puke –"

Chris swung the remaining shoe by the laces as he edged left and right, keeping the bastard's attention, angering him, looking for the right triggers and keeping the motion towards himself.

"You're scared of me I can tell, too scared to come and get me. What a pansy-arsed girl. Bring the knife to me and I'll show you what it's for, you puke-fucking shithole-licking twat-monkey cunt."

And in the flow of expletives that surprised even him, he calmed his breathing and let the moments fold up into one, throwing the unwanted, distracting thought of what a *twat-monkey* might look like away, so that he could focus, because the big guy had taken two steps and was hunched forwards, not centred at all. *Only a bit more*, Chris thought, then let fly suddenly on the next spin of the shoe without warning; the shoe's velocity wanting to escape the orbit of his fingers and doing so the moment he relaxed his grip. It hurtled upwards and clipped the side of the guy's head, not damaging but doing enough to make him recoil. Chris sprang forward and grabbed the knife arm from the inside, twisting and raising his hips so that the big guy stumbled right over him, centre of gravity completely lost, unable to stop himself or even swing the knife. With him defeated Chris could have a go at the others, who would be nothing to this guy – but he was yanked by a powerful fist, right off the edge, footing gone, disoriented. He punched out, confused, and the grip broke, but it was too late – they were both falling.

The Sea And The Cave

> "In the middle of the forest. There were wild mountain wolves and lions prowling ... poor bewitched creatures whom she had tamed by her enchantments and drugged into subjection." – Homer, *The Odyssey*

Out, out, wind rushing up at him; down, his kick at another falling shape connecting with a thud; he can't breathe as the cold air rushes into his lungs, not letting him exhale; wind blowing with enough power to gust him through the air, the chaotic darkness spinning, dreading the moment of crushing impact, teeth gritted; then he plummets past a white flash of wall, air all around, still alive. And suddenly the quality of sound changes, echoes, rock rushing past, he's over the cliff edge, spinning sideways, stone so close he can't believe he hasn't struck an outcrop yet as the world flips over and over in nauseating motion; a second later comes numbing impact with something hard, intense pain and then he is spinning away from the rock, soaring below, waves crashing, flying through spray –

– and an explosion of cold and pain that shocks him so that he can't believe his heart hasn't stopped; he gasps involuntarily and swallows water, eyes open to blackness, straining for breath, *which way is up?*, swimming up no, it's down, turn around, oh God need air, need air, hold on, against rock, half swimming half scrambling up it, slimy and sharp, slammed into it but head above water, coughing and puking burning liquid out but a holy gulp of air before being swallowed again by the icy rage around him, he knows which way is surface, and life, but feels his body moving down, sucked down with the sound all muffled, then spat up, shooting up in a huge wave until the sound has changed to a deafening roar and he knows to breathe again, again, again, trying to stay afloat as the water sucks, and it doesn't draw him down this time but pulls him out then flings him back at the rock; the water spreads and runs down but he can't; every bone is rattled by the force of the blow but he has to stay above the sea, not get slurped down into a vortex or be pulled under the lip of a submarine cave to drown. Must keep moving, keep moving along the rock to the left, ignoring pain and choking and cold; regular pattern of pulling him then slamming him back like a petulant child with a doll, he's so small, so small in the sea.

He battles against the fierceness, amazed that he is still alive, hasn't yet been smashed to tiny fragments wrapped in skin; the fight absorbs his mind now, the effort to survive, he can't live through a lunatic plunge like that just to die now.

His head hits rock with blinding force that makes Chris think of coconut shells being cracked. Everything goes foggy and he struggles to hold onto consciousness, his fingers hooked into a crevice with the barnacles, locked into position so hard that every knuckle cracks when he's forced to let go by the power of the next wave.

Then he can see it, a break in the rock, a beach, but the water is trying to rush past it, and he is going to be swept by, forty feet out, beyond the coastline, beyond any chance to live, his energy exhausted. He can't let that happen so swims as fast as possible, up and down on waves and sideways in currents, and he can hardly breathe and every muscle burns as the waves toy with him, and the nearer he gets to the shore the more rocks there are below, breaking the surface, jagged and black, but distorted by the huge tentacles of slimy seaweed which offer no protection when his knee or ankle or chest is thrown into them or torn on sharp protrusions. Then he is scrambling over slimy rocks, slipping on stinking wet seaweed, cutting his hands but not caring, now only waist deep, now knees, then he falls again, and doesn't bother standing.

But he can't rest; he crawls up the beach, gasping, clothes ripped, towards a cave, have to hide, have to hide, they will be coming.

Into the cave, arm sinking into a pool, slimy, something large and hard there, he pulls his hand back, moving as far from the entrance as he can, but it is pitch black.

When he can't go further he crawls behind a rock and curls up at the base on some wet sand, long slippery tendrils of seaweed against his body, too tired for disgust. He will stay awake all night, keep watch in case they come, keep watch for the big guy in red who may have hit the sea near him, and most of all keep watch for Megan in case she has been able to jump after all.

He was asleep in seconds.

Lord John stood by the altar in the chapel, dressed in the fine, black silk robes he wore only for special ceremonies. Where they folded a deeper black was created, representing the deepest shadows found on a full-moon night like tonight. The only other colour was the red trim on the hood which hung down at the back. Above him, the beasts carved into the timber roof grinned madly.

He was unaware of his observer; a dark figure watched from the shadows of the rounded arch that led into the chancel.

Lord John unscrewed the lid from the half-gallon plastic container, and dragged it to the side of the altar for easier access. The blood inside sloshed around thickly. The last parts of the ceremony could be performed here, and then he would wait for the messenger to herald ... whatever it would herald. It didn't matter that he didn't know the exact shape of the prize. To know its value was enough.

It also didn't matter that he hadn't heard from the islanders. The last few times he'd used the radio he had only received a screeching, wailing noise, which must have been interference of some kind. A minor irritation though. Wherever the few survivors had gone, they would have walked into a trap or ambush. If they'd gone to the first place he'd predicted – the lighthouse – then even turning on the radio would have closed the automatic shutters over the lights for a few minutes. His villagers wouldn't have missed that, out-of-control or not, and hopefully the temporary lack of a beam wouldn't have been noticed on the mainland. He had wanted to try out his idea of using the lighthouse as a trap ever since the General Lighthouse Authority had installed shutters a few years ago. They could be lowered during the day and the light mechanism turned off. Before that the lanterns had to rotate all the time, because the bullseyes were so powerful that if the mechanisms were still they would have acted like huge magnifying glasses and melted everything inside the top. As soon as the change to the system was made he had planned ways of using it to his advantage.

So he assumed the villagers had succeeded in their hunt; or maybe the Bwystfil had. In fact, it didn't matter now if the specially huge doses of his Turning elixir administered in the last black communion had turned their minds into molten slag, or their bodies into pockmarked husks. The after-effects might be brain death, madness, coma, amnesia, disease – it would give him lots of good data whatever the outcome. The main thing was that what needed to be done had been done, and he could –

The dark figure stepped forward into the light of the candles, the shadow from the box pews behind it now.

"Ah, you," said Lord John, momentarily startled by the apparition, having thought he was alone.

"*Ie. Fi.*" ["Yes. Me."]

"Not out with the others? It is not like you to miss out on the fun."

The beautiful girl took another step forward. "I don't like hunting very much."

"No, that's true. It never was your vice, was it? Your vice lies in other areas. Lies on your back most of the time, doesn't it, my dear?"

"I am not your dear."

"*Semper idem.*" Lord John gave her a look of disdain. "But I am your Lord still, aren't I?"

"You taught me about the Dark Ones. They are my Lords. They call to me."

"Oh, you are delusional. Truly you are."

"No! I'm not!" she snapped, her eyes reflecting the pinpoint orange of the candles. "The Harbinger, I am. Brân Ddu: The Black Crow! It's one of the few true things you told me."

Lord John sighed. "Are you, now?"

The girl was a simpleton. Her gullibility almost made him laugh; another yokel swallowing his sweetened concoction of truth and lies (and anything else put into her mouth for "religious" purposes). She was unable to discern which was which.

Maybe he should tell her. He would love to do that. Tell her the relic she worshipped was just a bone he had found washed ashore as a boy; part of the jaw of a whale or a big seal – not the relic of a Deep Dark One of the sea come to them. It was so stupid it was pathetic. She was no chosen one; her religion was a mishmash invented by him. Oh yes, he would love to tell her and see how the self-important whore took that: to see her face flow and melt as if he had used one of the failed hyperdermic compounds on her. But there was plenty of time.

"And why are you here now, Black Crow?"

"You didn't tell me what you were doing."

"Should I have?" the Lord asked sardonically.

"Yes! Yes, you should! I should have been told, consulted."

"You are not an oracle. Nonetheless, this is your complaint? That I didn't let you into all the details of what I was doing?"

She nodded.

"Let me tell you something, girl. Something about you, that may reveal your importance in the scheme of things." He smiled humourlessly at her, but she just glared back. "There is a plum tree at Plas Dof. Old, but still bearing fruit. The fruit of this tree seems rather appropriate now. You see, I have met girls who look pleasant, sweet and ripe, but they are disappointingly soft and squeamish, and have to be thrown away. Then there are most of the women of Pentref Bychan – shrivelled, with dried and cracked slug trails burnt onto their skins. And then there is you. So beautiful and firm on the outside. But at the end of the day you are just a plum – one that is blown with maggots inside, all wriggling below the surface. Black Crow? Harbinger? You foolish bitch! You're nothing but a dirty slut, Anne. Plain old Anne Jenkyns, the scabby whore with an English first name. You've belonged to *me* since your parents died. Now begone."

He turned away with an irritated swish of robes, sneering in contempt, not even wanting to waste his sight on her. As he did so she withdrew a short knife from a pocket in her skirt. With an animal snarl she leapt forward, eager to stab him. He heard movement and spun quickly, stepping aside with surprising agility. Then, with speedy assurance and a strange use of stresses and pitch he said coldly, "*Lamb**da** TAU* my *wOrd* is **lAw**."

And she stopped.

Her arms went limp and the knife fell from her grip with a clatter.

"I imagine you thought you would gut me with that," he said, kicking it aside. She remained motionless – the only life was the fire of hatred that burnt in her eyes.

"Oh, how the worm doth turn. My word is law, you know that – and yet you defy it?" Suddenly he yelled into her face, spittle flying from his lips, "And yet you DARE to defy me! To try to kill *me*!" He slapped her face hard, then stepped back and regained his composure.

Sweat broke out on the girl's forehead as she struggled for control over her body, a body which suddenly seemed to have become a hard shell holding her.

"Surprised? I wager it must be *so very disappointing* to realise I am this powerful. That I built control into you, as well. Then erased it from your memory. It is my use of words, you see. The tongue is mightier than the sword, one could say."

He picked up her knife. Her eyes focussed on it, but her body remained rigid.

"The question now is: what should I do?" He fingered the edge of the blade, angled it so that it glinted in the candlelight, in her full view.

"I should kill you, but that would be too easy. You amuse me, girl, and always have. It would be a shame for such a toy as you to be thrown away. I have also invested good time in your education, and it would be a pity to waste that."

He held the tip of the blade against her cheek, and pushed. Just enough to break the skin and start a drop of blood welling to the surface.

"It would be so easy. You can't even move away."

He let the blade glint once more in the light, then withdrew it with a regretful sigh. "There is no point disfiguring you either, your sour beauty might be useful to me. But you shall be punished. Lie down. On your back, the way you like it."

She struggled to do something else, to resist, and couldn't understand why her body obeyed him. Something so deep-seated, something uncoiling in a dark part of her mind that she'd thought was a dream ... She slowly lowered herself to the floor, limbs twitching, and lay back. The only things she could control were her eyes, and from them she glared, praying that she could kill him with a look, pour forth venom that would twist him and floor him and break this filthy control.

But whatever force moved her was too strong. Something had been done to her, but she could not work out what, or how.

"And now open your legs and pull up your skirt."

Hands that weren't hers moved to obey, revealing fair calves above her muddy shoes, then moon-pale thighs, separated by grey knickers. Tendons stood taut in her neck.

"Take off those knickers."

The Lord said it calmly, a peculiar air of sangfroid about him; even though her hands were not under her control, Brân Ddu found she could clench her teeth as her spirit rebelled. It felt like her body would break.

Lord John knelt and prodded her between the legs, as if examining a plate of food he suspected was well past being edible. He held the knife in front of her face.

"You wanted to use this on me, girl? Well, I could use it on you, now, and you wouldn't be able to stop me. Or I could make you use it on yourself. Except I think you would like that, you little silly slut. And I don't want to reward you. So what I want you to do is contemplate: think about how I could do anything to you. *Anything*. And this time ... I am going to let you go. After all, I am nothing if not forgiving of the follies of others. So like any merciful ruler I shall show clemency to those below me."

Still she clenched her teeth and fought, imagining her hands suddenly flying up claw-like to scrape out his eyes, to slam his head into the ground again and again, cracking it like a nut –

But it was no good.

"And I want to you remember this moment. It is a warning. You only get one." He rapped her on the forehead with the knife's handle as if to emphasise the point – it made a nasty hollow sound.

"I am your Lord and **lAw** is my *wOrd, kap***pa** *OMEGA*," he said, again with the strange cadence. "Get your worthless hide out of here, and don't ever cross me again."

Suddenly the locks in her joints snapped, control was hers again, and she scrabbled to pull her skirt down and get up. She snatched her knickers and rushed from the room without looking back, so that he wouldn't see her face.

She wasn't crying though, as Lord John assumed. Instead there was lightning behind her eyes – an inhuman thundercloud that had not yet burst. The storm was still there, and she told herself that when it broke, beasts would cower.

Grey light and agony.

He sat up in panic, at first unsure of where he was. Then panic *because* Chris remembered where he was.

He thought he'd heard a noise, and worried it was pursuers, but after waiting and listening he realised it was just waves sucking at pebbles.

Every muscle ached; every bone ached; every tendon ached.

He leaned back against the rock. Limpets jutted into him. Something spiny moved in the pool his hand had slipped into.

More light, still grey.

There were rips in his clothes, and green slime smeared on his knees and arms. Black strands of seaweed hung from a pocket, and green wavy ones that split into nodules rested across his bare feet. He wiggled his toes.

Examining his hands, then the skin below the rips in his clothes, he found swollen white cuts that stung but didn't bleed.

It hurt to breathe. He didn't look at his ribs. He knew they would be purple. At least one was probably broken. He hoped it was a small one.

He would have to move.

Joints cracked like whips as he got onto his hands and knees. One knee was swollen so much it was like kneeling on half a tennis ball. Using the rock as a support he got to his feet. The roof was low; he had to bend. His right ankle had trouble taking his weight. He hobbled towards the entrance like an old man, but as the roof grew higher so did he. The joints protested less and he stood upright and looked out onto the shingle beach.

No-one there, he thought with relief.

He scanned the sea's edge.

No-one there.

No-one ...

He limped to the edge of the sea and double-checked, looking for clothes, or marks of dragging, or anything.

A light drizzle was falling but the rain had stopped.

The storm was over.

The storm was over, but she wasn't there.

Grey light seeped in through the chapel windows, like dirty water spilling over the floor. It illuminated the dark patches of drying blood, pools of stinking shadow, sticky under Lord John's bare feet as he paced back and forth with wet slapping steps. The blood on the rest of his naked body was itchy; some bits smeared to a pale red, some crusted to a flaky claret that merged with thickened black.

What had gone wrong?

He thumped his fist down on the altar.

What had gone *wrong*?

Had all the years of study and prayer and calculation and corruption and sacrifice been in vain? All the stars and signs had suggested that last night would be a night of spectacular power.

Then nothing had happened!

Why? Had he done something wrong in the ceremony? Had he lost favour? Was some stupid word mispronounced or a rule of etiquette overlooked?

His body broke out in a cold sweat as a pain hammered through his head again. He groaned and fell to his knees in one of the cold and congealing puddles of blood, despairing. Lights flashed at the edge of his vision, the start of a migraine – something which had become more frequent in the last few years. Something his mother had suffered increasingly from before he'd had to put her out of her misery.

He beat his fist against the top of his head as if it would help and ground his teeth, before yelling curses at the empty chapel. They echoed back on him, hollow and unanswered. He squeezed his eyes tightly shut.

What could he do?

He could burn all the books that had misled him, for one. He actually grinned at that thought. Set fire to them all; teach them to mock *him*. A huge roaring fire to consume all of the falsehoods and ... start again, somehow. Rise from the ashes, a glorious phoenix.

How? How could he salvage this?

Now that he had a distraction his headache seemed to ease. He stood and paced again, searching for any spark of thought that could be fanned into something more useful. Something that could bring the light of hope into his darkness and dispel the depression.

His mind, his greatest gift.

Still functioning, calculating, so much stronger than any normal man's. He could use it.

What had he sought?

A prize. Despite all his gifts he had wanted more.

What if ...?

He lost the thought and tried to retrieve it before it disappeared forever.

What if ... what? What?

What if he had the prize?

That made no sense. Nothing had changed following the ceremony. He was the same as before.

He frowned in thought and a flake of blood peeled off his forehead and floated to the floor.

What if he had the prize already?

Still that nagging thought. Had the prize already?

Could that mean he had overlooked something?

All events had led to last night. It was meant to lead to a power or a realisation or ...

A realisation?

He *had* power. Power over many people, thanks to his studies and projects but ... something more ... he had sought more.

But what if he had been looking too hard at the grass of other fields, and missed that which was so good about his own?

A shock. A slap across the face.

That worked. That always made a silly bitch think again. Pain could make someone focus on *you*.

Pain was always given to others but ... he had received a shock last night, yes. A shock this morning, all one long shock ... and he had nearly despaired, given up, rather than look for meaning as any rational man would; look for lessons hidden.

So he had gone on a journey, and had received a shock. He was thinking now, using thought, why would he be shocked? Logic would suggest only two options. One was his first conclusion, that nothing had happened because he had been wrong. But maybe he had been *right*? Option two would be that he was being shown the truth of something, shaken until the message had sunk in. The message ...*what could it be?*

It was frustrating, this circling in his own mind, aware of a dark presence as he orbited round it but unable to see into the black hole, just spinning and becoming more aware of it by its effects. What could it be?

He paced even faster, unconsciously following the same route with such exactitude that there was an oval of smeared bloody footprints now, passing back and forth in front of the altar.

Slowly he tapped his palm against his fist as he walked and thought.

If he had a gift already, maybe he had been greedy for looking elsewhere? What should a parent do with a greedy and unappreciative child?

Shake it. Slap it. Dig nails into its arms. Make it cry until it appreciated what it had. Any good parent would do that.

And was he not a child before the Greater Powers? Perhaps he had been ungrateful too?

He had prayed for power when he had so many great gifts of intellect already, so much to be grateful for, surely it can't have all been a waste of time. He could not face that thought of such utter hopelessness. No. There had to be a reason.

He paced excitedly for some minutes until the chapel door banged open, breaking his flowering thought process. He turned angrily to see Wil dragging a woman in. Her hands were bound. She seemed to have given up struggling and half-crawled, half-staggered as he gripped her torn clothes tightly. Her bedraggled hair was stuck to part of her face but as they got nearer he recognised her.

The silly Megan Norris bitch.

Wil's eyes were glazed, and he seemed to have more trouble walking than dragging the girl, as if he was a dyspraxic strong-man.

"Well, well. Where did you get her, Wil?"

"At ... the lighthouse," he answered in a hoarse voice. "Brought her ... in truck."

"This is ... good," Lord John imitated, squatting before Megan.

She too seemed dazed and tired. Nonetheless she recoiled from his blood-caked nakedness and tried to pull away. But Wil's grip was tight.

"Hello again, Megan. You are lucky to be alive, do you know that?"

She glared at him, but he was pleased to see a respectful fear mixed with evident hatred and disgust. She looked away from his penetrating gaze.

Things were becoming clearer.

"You being brought here now is ... important. There is something in this that I need to ponder." He stood and pursed his lips. "Tell me, Wil – was she alone?"

"Yes. She was being dragged by group when I got there ... I brought her here."

"So where are your friends, Megan?"

She surprised him by answering.

"On their way to kill you, you bastard!" she spat with venom. "Unless you let me go they will come here and kill you! You bloody murderer! You did all this, didn't you?"

Lord John slapped her face and her bravado disappeared.

"Yes," he grinned. "I did."

What if they were alive too? That would be almost a miracle, wouldn't it?

"Wil, take her to the tomb. Secure her there. Then go back to the lighthouse and see what else you can find. Don't waste any time."

Wil shuffled away, dragging the sobbing woman.

And a new sense of purpose flooded through Lord John. There was a light in the darkness, and there were words in the light, and the revelation was close.

THE LAIR

> "But the sea-fowl has gone to her nest, the beast is laid down in his lair." – William Cowper, *The Solitude Of Alexander Selkirk*

Climbing the steep, slippery stone steps carved into the cliff was an agony of mind and body. Chris expected heads to appear over the cliff top above him.

They didn't.

Then, staying low, he crawled over to the bird-watching hut.

Listened.

Only the wind moaning through the weather-worn eaves.

He eased the door open, cursing the rusty hinges that shattered the natural peace, and his eyes adjusted to the darkness of the poky hut. It was empty. He entered and let the door close, moving to the viewing slits that faced inland. He raised one of the slats just enough to see out and watched for a few minutes: for any sign, any danger, anything suspicious.

Nothing.

He had hoped Megan jumped too. But if she had she would have either come to shore at the beach where he did, or she'd have drowned.

Maybe she had been captured instead of killed. He found it impossible to believe that she might have got away in some other fashion – she wasn't a fighter and this wasn't a film. But perhaps she was still alive for now. Not knowing the truth was the hardest thing.

All Chris wanted was to be somewhere safe. He could imagine how easy it would be – to sneak across the island using all the cover, to swim the waters that had hopefully receded now the worst of the storm was over; to make his way cautiously to civilisation and decide on the rest at that point. A warm bed somewhere, a hot bath; it was all so tempting. All he would have to do would be to head straight west. One foot in front of the other.

But he left the hut, gave one more glance down at the empty beach, then headed north-west, towards the lighthouse.

He moved from cover to cover, following the cliff edge, pausing often. Occasionally Chris cursed himself as an idiot – but he had been doing that for a lot of his life, and at least it made a change doing something idiotic in order to (hopefully) benefit someone else. Most of his idiotic behaviour in the past had been self-centred.

The sky was a sulky and spirit-dampening grey, but the breeze revived him, and once his muscles had warmed up he wasn't so uncomfortable. His leg and ribs ached, but he could ignore them. It was a pisser being barefoot – once when he trod on a thistle he could only just stop himself from yelling out – but he was so focussed on possible dangers he could mostly ignore his bare feet too.

He hoped he would find a clue at the lighthouse, or – even better in terms of being able to do something – Megan as a prisoner. Perhaps he would come across evidence that would settle the question of what had happened to her, but he didn't want to dwell on that.

Before long he reached one of the tracks that ran across the island; this one came from inland then followed the cliff to the lighthouse. He stayed off the track but remained near it as he moved, in case he saw anyone coming or going.

There was a payoff.

Just off the track, away from the cliff edge, was a boxy red Ford pickup at an angle. It seemed to have been driven through the bushes and come to a stop against a tree, but it couldn't have been a high speed collision because neither the tree nor the truck looked too damaged.

He recognised the truck: it belonged to Wil Griffiths, who ran the junkyard and garage. And he wouldn't normally lend it to anyone else.

After observing for a few minutes Chris was fairly satisfied there was no immediate danger nearby. No point putting it off any longer. He strode across the track and up to the vehicle. He reached the driver's door and looked in. Wil was there, head lolled to the side – dead, asleep or unconscious. Chris pulled the handle and the door opened with a loud creak. Wil didn't have a seatbelt on. Chris grabbed him by his thick, oil-stained shirt and heaved, dragging him out of the seat and throwing him to the ground. His Shell baseball cap fell off, revealing ginger hair. Wil groaned and started to stand, so Chris shoved him back with his bare foot. Wil's eyes opened and blearily focussed, and he tried to reach into the cab, aiming for a heavy spanner on the floor. Grabbing Wil's shirt, Chris wrenched him back from the cab, then, from behind, locked his left arm around Wil's throat, and held his own right bicep. His right hand forced the back of Wil's head forward, into the strangle. Wil gurgled and Chris yanked him further off balance, squeezing his left bicep even harder into Wil's throat. Frantically, Wil grabbed at Chris's arms but couldn't shift them. There was a stale smell, either old sweat or vomit, it was hard to tell. Chris squeezed tighter.

"You can't breathe you wanker. Stop struggling and I'll relax a bit."

After a few more seconds of resistance, Wil stilled, and Chris relaxed just enough to allow him to breathe, but not to the point where he couldn't slam the strangle on again immediately.

"I'm going to ask you questions, and you'll answer or I'll break your fucking neck, Wil. You understand?"

When there was no immediate reply, Chris applied the strangle hard for two seconds. When he relaxed it again, Wil was coughing.

"Understand, fuckwit?"

"Yes!" croaked Wil.

"Good. Is there anyone else nearby? And don't even think of lying. I'm not in the mood."

"No."

"So you're on your own?"

"Yes."

"Where's Megan?"

"Manor." Wil coughed again and Chris wasn't sure if he had heard him correctly.

"Where? Say it again."

"The Lord's ... mansion."

"Lord John?"

"Yes."

"You didn't kill her?"

"No. Took her ... there."

"Why?"

"Told to ... by Lord ..."

Wil started struggling again – it was so sudden that he almost broke free. Chris threw all his weight forward and applied the strangle, and this time he held as tightly as he could, keeping the pressure on until Wil collapsed – and then for a bit longer to be safe. Eventually he relaxed his grip and let Wil flop to the ground. There was crimson drool or sick dried below Wil's mouth, and he stunk. His eyes were red-rimmed. He looked more of a mess than usual.

"Silly fucker. I hadn't finished with you."

The Lord's manor, eh? He wasn't sure how much time he had, but there was none to waste.

He checked the truck; the keys were in the ignition. He hoped it would perform okay. Turning his attention back to Wil, he checked the pockets of his oily shirt and sagging tracksuit bottoms – empty. Wil's pulse showed he was still alive. Chris quickly compared his feet to the size of Wil's shoes, but he could tell they would be too small. Shit, he would have to be barefoot for a while longer.

Although it might have been a good idea to swap clothes, Wil's outfit was so ripe that Chris couldn't bring himself to. So he just picked up the frayed baseball cap and jammed that on his head. From outside the truck that would have to do.

And now, what to do with Wil? It was tempting to drag him to the edge of the cliff and throw him over, in case he came round and let anyone know that Chris was alive. Surprise was the only advantage he had. But to kill someone – especially someone who was unconscious ...

A scan of the truck's flatbed showed various tools, but nothing that would double as rope. Not even any gaffer tape.

"Looks like you're out of luck," said Chris.

Grabbing Wil under the armpits, he dragged his limp body over the track and past a few trees until they were at the edge of the cliff. Wil struggled when he was part-way there, coming round groggily. Chris sat him on the edge of the cliff and held his ankles.

"What are ... you doing?" gasped Wil, when he regained some level of consciousness.

Chris stood, lifting Wil's ankles so that he tumbled backwards over the cliff with barely time to yell before he had bounced off the rock and spun into the sucking sea. Chris watched his body bob around for a few seconds before it disappeared beneath a wave smashing against the base of the cliff. He was a goner.

He wasn't unconscious when I tipped him, Chris thought. *So I suppose I was only being half-bad.*

The truck started first time, and Chris reversed it out onto the track and drove south, towards the Lord's mansion and the village. Hopefully, he wouldn't see anyone else until he got there.

On second thoughts: hopefully, he wouldn't see anyone else then either.

Hunger gnawed at him, but the only thing in the glove compartment was half a packet of mints. He ate them as he drove, impatiently crunching them into white powder. That would have to do for now. There was no time to get food elsewhere. If possible he wanted to be in and out and long gone before he starved to death. So pushing thoughts of Chinese food out of his mind (and pizzas, and Indian food, and chips ...) he concentrated on the driving.

The truck bounced around on the uneven surface, seat springs squeaking in protest, but it covered ground quickly. Within ten minutes Coed Derwen bordered the trail and he was just north of the village. He had seen no sign of the islanders but although he'd been glad of that at first, he now couldn't shake the worry that it meant they were all back in the village.

That was the next decision he had to make. He could get out of the truck before joining the main road to the village and make his way to the Lord's mansion on foot. But if he were to be seen then, he would have fewer options. Also it would take a lot longer. Perhaps the best option was to stay in the truck and hope anyone glancing his way ignored it, assuming Wil was behind the wheel. Wil not only ran the garage on the main road, but he also owned the scrapyard behind it, and just beyond the scrapyard was the mansion.

Instead of thinking about it any more, in case he talked himself out of his plan, Chris just acted. He joined the road into the village, slowing the vehicle slightly. He didn't want to be so fast that he attracted attention – but just as importantly, he didn't want to be slow enough for any observers to get a look at his face.

There seemed to be no-one on the road. He turned right without indicating, opposite where he had driven off in the Subaru just over twelve hours before. Was it really such a short time ago when someone chucked a madstone onto the scales and tipped the balance from normality to chaos? Shit.

He was alert for anything – walkers, watchers, twitching curtains, another vehicle – but the place seemed as dead as the chapel graveyard. He hoped everyone was far away – or at least in the chapel – and his plan could work. Nonetheless, he *felt* as if he was being watched. Any movement and noise in the village was bound to be conspicuous.

No playtime bell rang in the dead school on his right; the dusty cracked windows just watched, jealous of the life they no longer contained.

The gate to the scrapyard was open and he swung in, bringing the truck to a halt with a crunch of gravel so that it faced the way out in case he had to leave in a hurry. He killed the engine, rolled down the window, and waited for a minute. From here he had a good view, through the chain-link fence, up the road, and also across to the school. The mansion was partly hidden by a pile of old rubber tyres next to a shed in the corner of the yard. Rusting hulks of tyre-less cars dotted the area, kept for no obvious reason.

No-one came. The shed door remained closed. Only the sound of a light pattering of drizzle on the truck roof. No bells, no shouts, no engines, no cutting machinery.

No excuse not to get out.

This was the point where he would have to ad-lib again. He grabbed the heavy spanner off the cab floor. He also removed the pickup key from the dirty bunch hanging out of the ignition and put it into his pocket, leaving the other keys that opened unknown doors on the floor.

Yanking the cap down and stepping onto the sharp gravel, he wished again for a pair of shoes. Hopefully, this wouldn't take long.

He ran out of the scrapyard and across the road. To his left was a six-foot grey stone wall surrounding the Lord's mansion, and Chris followed it towards the rear rather than going in through the main gate from the road. The wall was overgrown in many places, and beyond it he could see the side of the mansion.

He wasn't sure what determined whether something was a mansion rather than just an impressively large house – he suspected it was just the pretensions of the owner. That would fit with the little he knew about the pompous Lord.

The immense old structure seemed somehow strange. Perhaps it was all the sculptured elements which attracted the eye even as they created ominous shadows. Or maybe it was the impression it gave of having been designed from a mix of styles, as if several architects had been involved and had disagreed throughout the building process.

When he reached the back of the house Chris scrambled over the wall and dropped onto moss at the base of a dead oak tree. The walled garden was unkempt and neglected. Some distance away he could see graves and a tomb; their lonely and morbid aspect seemed fitting. The mansion was clad in a different grey stone from the walls, and had one square ivy-covered tower. In the breeze the ivy rippled like fur, contrasting with the still blackness of the reflecting windows which resembled hollow eyes. He hoped the eyes were dead.

Chris dashed across the open space and up some stone steps onto a narrow, white-balustraded porch. Spanner in his left hand, he gripped the iron ring handle on the sturdy, carved wooden door and turned it, and was surprised to hear the interior latch lift. He pushed the door and it opened with hardly any noise. Beyond was a narrow hall with two doors leading off. The hallway opened out through an archway at the end into a lavish-looking room. The floor was tiled with an intricate pattern of black and white triangles and the walls coated with a textured wallpaper, faded but expensive-looking, which ran down to the dark wooden skirting boards.

Still only silence.

He edged forward towards the archway. He didn't want to take the risk that the next door he opened might be a loudly protesting one. While stealth was on his side he would use it.

As he neared the carved archway, he saw more of the room beyond: some sort of sitting room with worn but comfortable-looking red leather sofas on islands of woven rugs against a sea of dark wood. To his left was a large stone fireplace that could have hidden two adults. Around the room were paintings – mostly portraits, but some strangely-painted landscapes too – and the room was dominated by a wooden staircase which curved upwards. A grandfather clock ticked in the corner, the only sound. Then came a creak and a hiss and suddenly sharp pain exploded in the middle of Chris's back. He staggered and looked back down the corridor to see Lord John, grinning, holding what appeared to be a long-barrelled, black pistol.

"Bullseye! Good job I have been practising my aim, eh?"

Chris started towards him but the room seemed to move and he had to lean against the wall for support. Keeping his grip on the spanner, with his other arm he tried to reach up his back to where the pain was. His fingertips touched what felt like a plastic dart embedded in the flesh to one side of his spine.

"Don't worry, it shouldn't be fatal. Just a little dose of veterinary-quality Thiopental. I have to admit that I put you down as a half-ton heifer, for my own safety – no insult intended!"

"Muffa-fuckar," Chris muttered, his tongue feeling like it was swelling up. His vision swam. He slumped to the floor.

"It will cut short your tour I am afraid – but one room out of the twenty-eight will have to suffice. It is more than many people see. And it was a most unexpected tour I have to say – but later on we will get acquainted with each other. *Very* acquainted. And you can then tell me in lots of detail what you are doing here, Chris Jones."

Chris used all his reserve of willpower to crawl forwards, but everything was tunnelling into a long black tube, telescoping, the only bit of light at the end of which echoed and was accelerating away from him so fast he felt motion-sick. The last words he heard – "And by the way, welcome to my ancestral home, Plas Dof." – were muffled as he fell forwards.

Chris woke to a faint smell of urine. Mouth dry and head aching, he wondered where he was. Must have been quite a bender he'd been on. His eyes were sticky when he tried to open them.

For some reason he couldn't move his hands to help out his eyes. As if they were restrained, somehow. He was hungry and his stomach felt hollow. When he eventually opened his eyes there was only darkness. He was sitting in a chair instead of lying in a bed.

Once it all clicked together and he remembered how he had got here – *wherever here was* – he realised that he was in deep shit.

Well, at least he wasn't dead yet.

He struggled against the bindings but they were tight. As he moved his fingers around, he guessed they were some kind of straps, maybe leather, and a cold touch of metal may have been the edge of a buckle. His chest seemed to be restrained by a strap as well.

A noise came from beside him. A brief scuffle. He stopped struggling and listened. The scuttling noise had sounded stealthy. Possibly claws of some kind.

Staying as still as possible, quieting his breathing, he listened for any further noises. He also looked around, hoping his eyes would adjust but they didn't, even after what felt like five minutes – so there was no light at all.

Complete silence again. The stealthy movers were perhaps watching him from the cold blackness. He wasn't sure which was worse – noises of other *things* he couldn't see; or the disembodied feeling of floating in space, alone. Then, just when he was about to resume his struggling, he heard a sound that made the hair on his neck prickle. It was like a swallowed gulp, this time from somewhere behind him, followed by a moan that sounded almost human before it rumbled back into nothingness.

He held his breath. When no further noises came – and his head wasn't ripped off from behind – he called out, "Hello, is there someone else in here?" His voice sounded like it was reflecting off hard surfaces.

His reply came immediately, another gulp, a sob perhaps, and a sound that resembled chains being moved. It was almost enough to freak Chris out, but he told himself to remain calm, not least because there was nowhere he could go and little he could do.

"If there is someone else in here let me know."

From the darkness came throaty sobbing, a gurgled utterance that may have been, "Help me."

Oh Jesus Fuck, thought Chris, but aloud he asked, "Is that you, Megan?"

From the blackness no sensible sound came to confirm or ease Chris's fears; and as he tried rewording his question in different tones to get a response, there was a new distraction: a noise of grinding metal ahead of him, followed by a metallic creak and a waft of different cold air. A beam of torchlight moved from the floor to his face, blinding him. It stayed there for a few seconds before being turned off, its bearer apparently satisfied.

There was a click and a buzz as long fluorescent strip lights flickered on, and Chris had to close his eyes at first, everything seemed so blindingly bright after the complete absence of light.

"I see you're awake, Chris Jones. Interesting, you should have been out for a while yet. You must have a good constitution. Excellent." Chris recognised Lord John's pompous and slightly effeminate voice straight away. A squeak of hinges as the door was closed. Chris opened his eyes a slit, acclimatising them as quickly as possible. There was a rattle – things on a tray.

"I have to say it was kind of you to visit. You really should use the front door next time though, otherwise you might get mistaken for a thief. Is that what you are?"

Chris tried to calm himself.

"Don't want to talk, eh? That's fine, there will be plenty of time for that. You were good, quite stealthy, but you should have parked further away. Wil's vehicle was the first noise I'd heard for some time – you must have noticed how deathly quiet everywhere is – so it was bound to attract my attention. It was quite amusing actually, watching you run about outside."

Chris could now see vague shapes, including Lord John's blurry outline as he moved around.

"Do you *know* why you're here?" asked Lord John.

Chris remained silent, thinking, adjusting. He was certain that asking to be released wouldn't get him anywhere.

Something scraped as it was picked up off a tray; Lord John moved closer, to Chris's side; a switch was flicked.

Sudden pain in his arm, heat and vibration and stinging as muscles contracted, his eyes flew wide open despite the brightness and his back arched. It only lasted a second but his teeth seemed to vibrate afterwards. He was glad he hadn't bitten his tongue. Lord John stood there in some kind of old lab coat holding what looked like electric hair clippers that trailed a black cable.

"I don't like being ignored, Chris. This is a nice little tool for getting people's attention. Think of it as a portable, handy cattle-prod for humans – or as a talk-persuader, I don't care – but when I speak to you, you *will* answer, or this will happen again. It's on the mains you know, so there is plenty of juice.

"Well that's your warning; heed it. I suppose it doesn't really matter why you think you're here at the moment. We'll get to that. Other tasks to do first."

Lord John put the electric shock device on a trolley and turned away to work with some containers and equipment on a surface nearby. He was humming happily to himself. Chris took the opportunity to look around.

Brick walls, painted white but peeling, a feeling of age and decay. Strip lights. Ahead an old metal door set into the wall, presumably heavy, judging by the noise it had made on opening. There was an old-fashioned closed-circuit camera bolted to the wall above the door.

He was strapped into what resembled a dentist's chair by two tight wrist straps and a thick, cracked leather strap across his chest. His legs and head were free but he couldn't stand or turn.

Around the room were small animal cages, the kind he would have expected in a lab. He assumed some had rats in, which would explain the scuffling he'd heard first.

Twisting further he could see a much larger cage behind him, which reminded him of a zoo pen with straw on the floor. Inside the cage was the source of the other noises in the dark – a man in a ragged T-shirt but otherwise naked. Or what was once a man. Now the face was so disfigured that it looked more like dirty pink chewing gum, stretched then hardened in the sun. Reddened eyes stared out of the mess back at him, then the man raised an arm which ended in a stump rather than a hand and moaned something unintelligible.

Chris faced the metal door again and tried not to vomit. His face felt hot. Maybe a hot face was what happened instead of being sick when your stomach was empty.

Just think of that, anything to distract from the contents of the cage ...

Lord John finally approached Chris with one hand held ominously behind his back.

"Megan," Chris said, staring Lord John in the eye. "Megan Norris. Where is she?"

"Where *is* she? A good question. Is she why you *think* you came here? Don't tell me you thought you would rescue her? Is she good in bed and you want a bit more? Surely you have more immediate worries than some silly woman?"

"Where the fuck is she!" Chris yelled suddenly, making Lord John flinch. He obviously didn't expect to be shouted at.

Lord John recovered himself with an irritated look. "You will find out soon. Don't be such a bore."

From behind his back, he revealed a syringe. He waved it hypnotically in front of Chris's vision. Chris clenched his teeth.

"Well, that shut you up, I have to say."

"Don't inject me," said Chris, head lowered and gaze directed at Lord John from beneath bony brows.

"These are such amazing tools. The power to heal or to hurt." Lord John squeezed the plunger down slightly, and the tiniest spurt of liquid arced from the tip and onto the floor.

"Don't you fuckin' inject me." Chris's voice was louder now. He hoped it projected threat rather than fear.

Lord John smiled and held Chris's nearest forearm, moving the needle tip along the skin until it reached a point next to the strap and he seemed satisfied with the placing. Chris wriggled and tried to pull his arm back but the straps were so tight that he hardly even had feeling in his hands.

"If you move the needle might snap."

"Don't inject me, whatever it is don't do it, we'll work this out some other way!"

Lord John smiled a seemingly benevolent smile before pushing the tip of the needle under Chris's skin and slowly depressing the plunger.

The Turner

"Fear not the future, weep not for the past." – Percy Bysshe Shelley, *The Revolt Of Islam*

"Now I'm going to leave you for a while."

"What have you injected me with?" Chris was torn between fury and apprehension; between the need to know and the fear of knowing.

"I'm feeling generous, so I'll tell you. Double N-Dimethyl-tryptamine is a methylated indoleamine-derived serotonergic extract from the *Prestonia amazonica* plant. You're no wiser for knowing though, are you, so why ask? I'll refer to it as DMT in future; I'm sure you can remember that."

"You bastard, what does it do?"

"You wouldn't understand even if I told you. I will let you off for swearing again this time, though it is becoming tiresome. Enjoy the next forty-five minutes."

Ignoring Chris's mixture of demands for information and colourful curses, Lord John left the room – leaving the light on – and the heavy metal door thudded into place with a decisive echo.

Oh fuck.

How had his life gone downhill like this? It felt as if he were falling, or lurching drunkenly. But was that because of the stuff from the needle, or was it a normal response to a fucked-up situation?

He struggled, tugged, tensed, fought against the straps until his biceps bulged and the veins stood out, but it only left him feeling weak, frustrated and dizzy.

A small droplet of blood was growing where the needle had entered his body. *In some ways a beautiful red, crimson, energy of life – but perhaps a beauty that isn't meant to be seen, which is why it darkens and crusts.*

That was a weird thought to pop into his head. It didn't feel like something that belonged there. Like the stuff in his bloodstream, it was intimately unwelcome.

Chris had been in A&E a few times for stitches to deep wounds, and always refused anaesthetic. He didn't like the associations that needles created in his mind. He wondered if this syringe had been a new one or not. Lord John hadn't even wiped the jabsite first, so maybe other things were being done wrong too?

Chris laughed aloud at that, things were so obviously "being done wrong", and his laugh echoed sharply and unpleasantly. "Testing, testing," he said – again the echo, but also a dullness in his ears, as if they needed to pop. Like pressure when driving along mountainous roads. Driving along steep-sided green valleys – probably Welsh – leading here, to this place, this time, this situation.

Searching for ideas, he turned round as much as he could, towards the cage. The deformed man within was slumped; he looked dead. He also had a slight red haziness around him, which must be a trick of the light.

"Oi, mate!" Chris called. "Can you hear me?"

But there was no response, and it ached to twist round like that, so he turned back.

The drop of blood seemed darker. He wanted to wipe it away, an urge that became all the more irritating because he couldn't. He couldn't even lean forward to look at it properly. Darker red. No, not just that. Were the walls darker? No, they were lighter, as if the bulbs had gone up a few watts. But they left a blur when he moved his eyes. He checked it again, shifting his eyes left, right, up, down, in circles; oh yes, it blurred all right, after-traces.

Then he regretted moving his eyes so much, since the appearance of the spinning room made him dizzy. Or maybe the stuff in him did. He didn't feel normal.

What was normal?

What a laugh – sodding ironic – he'd never bothered with drugs, most people he knew who used or dealt were either tools or unreliable, or it went wrong. Not a good thought when here he was, strapped in with the dose of MDMA, or MMA, or whatever shit it was, making him feel sick and high. At a time when he needed to think clearly, think and plan and play it safe. Use the faculty he had which junkies didn't.

Who was he kidding though?

That wasn't his thought, and he shook his head violently to dislodge it.

"No room at the inn, mate. Fuck off!"

Now it sounded as if his ears were blocked, padding and distancing him from real sounds, big cauliflower ears of cotton wool. What if they really looked like that?

He kept losing focus. He had to stay with it.

Look round, the dirty cages and shiny trays – didn't smell so bad in here now, more like oranges than piss and shit – with shiny things on, something useful there, something sharp, or he could stick the zapper up Lord John's tight arse and make him dance, do the lo-co-motion, oh shit –

He was laughing again at the imagery; he could almost picture it happening, with spasmodic leg and arm movements from the little bastard as he danced.

But the glare from the buzzing (if muffled) lights cut into his eyes painfully and he was back in the room. As that hypnotist would say, "Don't look around the eyes, look into the eyes. You're under. Chris Turner you're a prat, and when you wake up you'll realise this and start thinking seriously about how to get out of the deep shit you're in, even if it smells of oranges, it is deep shit; oh, and you don't want the lobster, three, two, one: you're back in the room."

Bollocks. He couldn't hypnotise himself. If he could, he'd try to stop the feeling of being so weak and light that he could float away like a bubble on the wind. How long had it been since Lord John left? Ten minutes? Twenty? More? Even that wasn't something he could answer. Useless.

He snapped at the wrist straps again and again, but he could barely feel his fingers. Too tight. Too tight to fight. All right.

"Shit!" he yelled, the sharp muffling echo hardly letting him hear his own voice – the invisible cotton wool presence watching and absorbing sound; if he sank any more he would be asleep. "Shit, shit, shit!"

So much frustration, he hadn't felt that since, since ...

Since his sister died?

"Oh-ho now! Fuck off, voice, this is *my* head!"

Did he say that in his head or aloud?

But it was true. No matter how shitty things got, he always had options, something he could do. But not now. And not then.

He slumped, defeated.

Fuck, he didn't want to think about that. But it was as if his mind had found something to focus on and wouldn't let go. As he pushed the thoughts away it just seemed to embrace them, give them more prominence, more power.

He realised his eyes were shut. When had he closed them? He opened them but it was too bright.

He closed them again and it was too dark, but at least that way his head didn't ache behind the eyes. His eyes needed to rest, and his brain was cushioned with them closed, no way in for the outside world. Just him in the dark.

But what was in his brain? Fuck, he didn't want to know!

His sister was there again, in his head with him. Intimate, like a real presence.

He didn't want to think of her. Not now when he needed to be strong and focussed. Not ever.

And he felt guilty, as if she were looking at him, appearing as she did when she was younger, and softly accusing: *Why would you keep trying to forget about me? Didn't I love you? Shouldn't you remember me?*

Especially if you let me down?

Sad brown eyes, they wrenched his heart like a gut punch. Worse – hell, worse – a bloke could punch him in the head but he'd stay up, and grin through the bloody split lip, intimidating his attacker; but there was no honour in wounds inside, wounds that only you could deal with.

Was there any honour in him anyway? Did he give a shit about the answer to that one?

No. But he did give a shit about protecting people who trusted him.

And so it came to this at last, strapped down so he couldn't run, not from the law and not even from memories; his eyes shut against the dirty wonderland outside, but unable to hide from what was here in his head with him.

"That you, Jezzie?"

He didn't care if that was out loud or just to himself as long as she heard it.

She smiled and he knew it was her. Curly dark hair, her coffee skin a different tone from his because, although they had the same mother, by the time Jezzie was born he had a new dad called Antwon, with black skin. It didn't matter to Chris that he and Jezzie looked different. She was his little sister, and everyone in the red-brick, new town estate soon learnt that if they upset Jezzie then her wild brother with the heavy fists would be there. A guy who made her cry would pay the tears back, and a girl who'd bitched at her might find her boyfriend pissed off, sporting a black eye and snapping at her to leave the fucking Afro girl alone in future.

Yeah, when Chris was around no-one touched Jezzie. It was as if his mission in life was to look out for her. Even when she occasionally got pissed off at his overprotective big brother act, he liked to believe that she was still secretly pleased. He didn't want anyone hurting her. There was enough hurt in the world, and once he had someone to love and who was worth protecting from the shit, he would keep on flushing the chain so she didn't have to deal with it.

That's what he wanted. She knew that because she was still smiling at him in his head, still Jezzie at her best, the sister he adored.

But that hadn't been enough, had it? He had a reputation, and got involved with things and people that were more addictive than the drugs that always seemed to pervade that world, influencing people and plans and money.

Well, that shit's history, no point going there. What happened, happened. He felt tense, his mouth dry – *his own* past was not important.

Jezzie smiled at him; it was a sharp knife, stiletto-like in its ability to puncture his inner organs while leaving no visible wound on the outside. Only she could do that.

you couldn't always be there for me

I should have been. I should've dragged you away from the fuckhead wasters you mixed with. Kicked the shit out of them and locked you up till you were straight like I'd tried once before, even though you said it made you hate me *it did, then, but I was wrong*

but even so, I should have done it, since you wouldn't listen to me, not really – you always agreed and then you'd be fucked off your head again when I tracked you down

you did the best you could

I could have done more

how?

I could

how could you have done any more when you were in prison for so long?

"Fucking hell! I want to go! Fuck it all and let me out of here!"

Chris was crying, and he couldn't even put a hand over his face to hide it, couldn't keep the tears behind his lids, he was leaking – that's all it was, leaking.

I always loved you, big brother, you and me – both fuckups in our own ways.

"I love you, Jezzie, I'll save you when I get free."

Snotty nose, sniffling like a kid *I know you do I love you too* and it's all fucked up, this whole world –

He fought back nausea but the tears were harder to subdue, and when he opened his eyes and screamed she was still there for a second, smiling, then just a brown after-image against the glowing walls; everything had a glow or an aura but hers was the only one worth seeing. It faded before his eyes, and even though there were muffled noises from the cage behind him (*words, Chris, someone speaking*) he blocked them out because he only wanted to hear more from Jezzie; real or not, she was the most alive he'd seen her since she died and he prayed that it was really her and not something to do with the blurred room or the feeling that his body was stretching away from him. *She said she loved me*;it had been her,

and he let himself cry even though he knew she wouldn't be back

and he cried

and time passed

and he stared up at the camera

and waited.

"Still with us, I see," Lord John said breezily when he eventually returned, wearing his most sociable smile. "From the look of your face I assume you have had some adventures while I have been gone. Why don't you tell me what happened?"

"I need a piss," Chris growled.

"Do it in your trousers then. What happened?"

"I farted."

"You are an obstinate and scatologically-obsessed Neanderthal," Lord John replied without malice, refusing to be stirred. "I *know* you're lying. Ten to fifteen minutes after I left the room the DMT will have reached its peak effect. Concentration tends to fall rapidly to baseline levels after that as your body processes it – I imagine it is hardly detectable by now. But at the peak – I would *really* like to know what was going on in your head."

"Fuck off and die."

A momentary pursing of the lips before Lord John resumed his magnanimous smile. "I'll find out later. I have a long list of possible effects, distortions, perceptive disturbances, emotional reactions and hallucinations, but the content and subject's interpretation is of interest. I watched you on the camera – less obtrusive to your delirium – but it only shows me the *outside*. However, it is an understanding of the *inside* that leads to control.

"You must be hungry – many people end up with so-called 'munchies' – and I have a snack here." He rummaged in a leather bag and produced a white-bread sandwich, held up so Chris could see the freshness of it, some moist filling with green lettuce jutting over the edge. "And you can have it if you tell me."

The ravenous hunger within Chris woke up fully, gnawed at his insides like a starving wolf. He hadn't eaten anything proper in over 24 hours, and even if he hadn't been so physically active he would be almost ready to kill for a plate of chips and beans by now.

"I'm not hungry," he said. His stomach immediately growled in protest, a traitor to his will.

"No matter. I'll find out later." Lord John munched on the sandwich. The bread looked so soft, the lettuce so crisp ... Chris's mouth watered.

At least it got rid of his dry throat, he told himself sourly.

Speaking as he ate, in an uncharacteristically impolite way, Lord John said, "I admire you. I know it may seem strange for someone like *me* to say that I admire someone like *you*, but it is true. Because you are so *stubborn*. And you aren't what you seem. The more I find out, the more certain I am that this was meant to be. I suspect you of having a criminal past, though I haven't been able to pinpoint any details yet. But the evidence fits, and it is only a question of which happens first – me piecing it together using my sources and finding the right records – or you cracking and telling me. Because I assume you will be reticent on that subject too?" By now he was down to a piece of crust and popped that into his mouth as well.

"I don't mind talking a bit," said Chris.

"Really?" asked Lord John with a raised eyebrow. "I'm surprised again. Go on."

"You're close enough, you freak. Yes, I've got a past. I wish I didn't. I wish I'd never broken the law. I wish I'd never heard of this obscure shithole. I wish I'd run somewhere else. And – most of all, top of the list – I wish I'd snapped your scrawny neck the first time I saw you."

"Your real name?" asked Lord John curtly, the condescending smile gone.

"Only for friends or Governors. Or when it doesn't matter any more."

"Oh, it doesn't matter any more."

"Where's Megan?"

"Back on that topic?"

"Where's Megan?"

"Tiresome."

"Where's Megan?"

"Change the record, Chris."

"Where's Megan?"

"If you –"

"Where's Megan?"

"Shut up!" Lord John snapped. "You can try the patience of a saint, you know that? I don't like to lose my temper – I sometimes do things I regret afterwards."

A pause.

"Where's Megan, dickweed?"

"Right! I'll let you see the scraggy bitch." Lord John turned and strode to the metal door, which he'd left ajar. "I was keeping her company while you were tripping the light fantastic. Megan, come and say hello to Captain Caveman."

Lord John opened the door wider. It made a grating squeal that could set anyone's nerves on edge, and he stuck his head through the gap into the darkness beyond. Chris stared, and tried to fist his hands but they were numb.

"It's all right, Megan, you can come in. You're among friends now." Lord John spoke as if encouraging a child. "Why are you being so shy? Here, let me help you –" He reached through the gap and appeared to pull.

Chris tensed, body still but heart beating fast, as close to a physical prayer as he ever got.

"Stubborn, aren't you? Come on girl, don't be such a prima donna, you look wonderful."

Again there was, seemingly, resistance as he pulled; he opened the door wider, reached through with both arms, and pulled again unsuccessfully. Lord John turned to Chris with an apologetic and bemused look. "I don't know what you see in her ..." and he pulled harder as if tugging a reluctant person, and did a theatrical turn into the room, his arms holding something by the hair,

it was just a head

something rounded and red raw at the bottom

Megan's head

with a face.

"Things have come to a head now, haven't they, girl?" cackled Lord John as he held Megan's remains out by fingers gripped in her matted hair, one of her eyes closed and bruised and the other open but sightless, the mouth agape and bloody and the neck torn and ragged.

"Since you pushed me so, I have given in, so here she is. She's lost some weight – silly dieting sort-of-a-girl, perhaps – but she could certainly turn someone's head. Don't be shy, woman, say hello to Chris; he's been dying to see you again!"

Chris ground his teeth like stones in a mill, looking away from the monstrosity held out before him by a maniac.

He'd failed again.

"You're dead," he stated with finality.

"Are you saying that to me or to her?" asked Lord John. "I suspect anything you say will be over her head. But you see, I *said* she wasn't why you are here, despite what you thought. So there must be another reason. I'll tell you what it is, because I want you to be a willing part of all this, since it will make things easier on both of us. So I'm going to explain. She can listen too, as long as she promises not to bite my head off." Lord John placed the torn remains of Megan's neck on the top shelf of the stainless steel trolley nearby. It took two attempts to keep it from rolling over. Her drained face looked slack and artificial. Chris let his gaze fall downwards.

"Are you sitting comfortably?" Lord John asked. A scrape of a chair as he sat down and stretched his legs out. "Then I'll begin.

"Where to start? It all revolves around Turning, if you'll pardon the pun – a hobby of mine for so long, and something I only saw as a means to an end, but since then I have realised I was wrong. It can be so much more, an end in itself – and it has been all along.

"But I'm getting ahead of myself. My original obsession was the occult. I've studied all the books, you know. With their help I convinced myself that someone who sacrificed enough – and performed the correct rites – would gain fantastic power. I did all that, and –" Lord John clenched his right hand into a fist, his voice rising in pitch, "– nothing happened! A damp squib! It just became ridiculous, standing there naked and chanting to an empty chapel. I was up to my arms in blood, and wondering – had I got the date wrong? *Again*?"

Chris kept his gaze low so that he didn't look at Megan's accusing face.

He needed time. The prick wanted to talk so he would let him. He might find out something useful – or at least delay for a while whatever the arsehole had in mind.

"Oh, I was angry, as you can imagine. Furious! There were tears before bedtime, I admit. All the death, destruction and harvesting of souls. Today was to be my day of glory."

"But it wasn't," humoured Chris.

"Wrong!" said Lord John, triumphantly. "It was. It *is*, but in a different way. After the tears and curses, I had a vision of loveliness. I came to my realisation, my true understanding of the journey that Turning has taken me on. I realised that I already *had* the power I sought, something to work on! No more playing around for me.

"Megan was a help in that, triggering some of the thoughts, leading to ideas, possibilities. I knew she could be a useful piece in the game, though at that point I hadn't decided how to use her. So I left her to one side. And then *you* came along, like a proof, if one were needed. Perfect in the way you appeared and got my attention. I could see my fate in you, a chance to perfect things. And so I sacrificed a piece in the game, and I hope it was worthwhile in showing you that there is no hope in confronting me, no chance of escape. No-one to rescue. Just you and me, with no distractions, and your only choice being between the hard road and the *very* hard road.

"So, returning to my point – I *did* get a power – the power of vision, and I intend to keep the faith. I cried tears of gratitude then, for my power was the perfect ability to see the world as it truly is, to see *possibilities*. And one way was to save Turning for strong people. Everyone else is just entertainment. I see new processes before me, perfected on new subjects. You are exceptional, Chris, a survivor, a man of power, and I'm going to use you. I'm going to break you and remake you, and convert you into something different. Something even better. I want you to share this glory."

"You had better tell me more then." Chris marvelled at how someone as mad as Lord John had been around for so long. "What's this 'Turning' bollocks you keep mentioning all about?"

"It's a form of psychological conditioning. Modern conditioning methods date back to the 1950s. The CIA ran a number of projects – and still do, according to many. The most well-known are projects with innocuous names such as 'Artichoke' and 'Bluebird', both from the early 1950s, with the charming aims of controlling individuals to the point where they would do the Government's bidding against their will – and even against such fundamental laws of nature as self-preservation. The technology used was developed by the well-known CIA psychologist, John Gittinger. The A-Treatment, which I have adapted, was first created by him.

"However, what they did had been done by others already. You see, this whole lab has been fitted out by me, but the secret area itself was built by one of my ancestors. I found it when I was fifteen, during a summer in which I read my deceased Great Uncle Philip's diaries. He had been extremely obsessive and paranoid; his diaries were written in obscure languages, and often in code, so translating them had become a hobby of mine. I found the progression of my Great Uncle's descent into madness fascinating, it was like being in his head. I learnt many things about the house and family, including the existence of this secret complex and the location of its key.

"I later realised that Great Uncle Philip wasn't the only member of my family to have had secret cupboards or rooms. The mansion is riddled with them, and I suspect that I only know the locations of half, because so many ancestors carried their secrets to the grave. But I was glad I had this one.

"Great Uncle Philip hadn't built it – the diaries were clear on that – but once Philip found it he had continued with the one project that united many of our family, the ones I think of as Realists. What was always referred to as Turning.

"Obviously they worked in a more primitive way than I am capable of, with my hi-tech and extremely expensive and reliable equipment. It was me who took Turning to new heights, me who got it to work like my ancestors would never have believed. They had got close, but I have gone right through the bullseye and into its brain.

"Of course, their old ways of Turning worked to a degree. They followed the *right* order of things, from the obligation to the kowtow to obedience, the natural progression; then on to suggestion, fear, indoctrinated clinical xenophobia, hypnotism – Great Uncle Philip had apparently been a dab hand with a swinging fob watch – financial control, bribery, induced madness, ritual, social pressure, superstition manipulation, moral corruption. And the great one – sex – which I have continued to use where appropriate, despite my personal lack of interest in rubbing my private parts against other people like a primitive. Sex has always worked well on others as a means of corrupting and creating loyalty, and islander-only orgies combined with black masses made a good combination, especially when I let the men rape some woman they had caught. And in the absence of raw material like that, I could usually rely on Anne – the whore I corrupted into loving it, and being loyal to me, and of whom you are no doubt aware. It wouldn't surprise me if she has opened her scrawny legs for *you* too. No need to answer that, just an idle thought. Well, I told her it was power – which was true, but not power for *her*, as the silly bitch believed – it was power for *me*.

"Sorry, that makes me sound a tad egocentric, doesn't it?

"Most women are less useful because they are harder to Turn for some reason, sex apparently being less of a motivator for them. So most of the other women are just beaten into submission until they are too scared to intervene, with rape as a tried and tested form of breaking-in if necessary. No-one could say that their Lord was unfair though – the women are given the right to stay out of it or get involved as the fancy takes them. And the fancy *did* take some of them, who joined in, and sometimes persecuted victims worse than the men! I have copious notes on these effects. The bullied always make the best bullies when they are thrown a victim, I have found, and I imagine you have come across that behaviour too, Chris?"

"Maybe."

"This is jolly, isn't it? I almost regret being mean to you now. Are you thirsty?"

Chris was. The dry throat was back; he had ignored the headache caused by dehydration, but he knew it would only get worse. He needed his strength, and humouring the wanker might be a good ploy.

"Yes. Can I have some water?"

"Of course you can. If we are civil to each other things go much smoother, don't they?"

Lord John reached into the leather bag, apparently oblivious to Megan's head nearby. Chris wished *he* could be. Lord John withdrew a thermos flask and poured water into the cup.

"Will you untie me so I can drink it?" asked Chris.

Lord John pursed his lips in a manner that resembled a warning. "Just because I'm being nice doesn't mean I'm a fool."

He held the cup against Chris's lips and tilted it so he could swallow greedily. The water felt beautiful and refreshing, a simple pleasure amidst all the horror.

He contemplated biting Lord John or doing *something* positive, with him being so close – but decided it was futile, so just drank the life-giving fluid. At that moment, it tasted nicer even than whisky.

Lord John returned the cup to the top of the thermos flask, as if this were a pleasant picnic rather than the prelude to something that was undoubtedly going to be painful, horrible, and possibly fatal for Chris.

"Anyway, back to the main story, since I am quite warmed up and enjoying this – are you comfortable too?"

"Not really. My hands are dead."

Lord John examined them. "Oh yes. Scarcely any circulation. We wouldn't want them to turn necrotic, would we?"

"No, we wouldn't."

"Very well, I'll loosen them one hole. But don't even *think* of trying anything. If you move an inch while I loosen the strap then I'll zap you until you pass out – or fry, whichever comes first. And when you come round you will find the straps tighter than before. Understood?"

"Yes."

"Excellent."

Lord John loosened the strap on Chris's left hand. The skin was swollen and red where it had cut into him. His hands had been numb for so long he knew they would be useless. Much better to get some feeling back in them and maybe have their use later. It wouldn't hurt to stay in Lord John's good books for now, either. So throughout the process Chris remained completely still, fully aware of Lord John's readiness to flee at the slightest movement. When Lord John returned to his seat Chris still failed to move his fingers, but could see that the straps were less cutting than before.

He would have one hell of a case of pins and needles.

"Well, time presses on and there is much to do. You know most of it now. What my ancestors had done. But I had three distinct advantages over them.

"Firstly, I am the last of the line. So there are no disagreements and in-fighting to direct attention away from perfecting the process of Turning; no-one else to drain money away from that goal. The disagreements used to get to me, but after I had tested various procedures on my mother and cousin there were no more disagreements. Not because the process had worked, but because it proved fatal to them. Those were early days in the research, after all.

"Some of my early experiments were useful though. The processes I used on the being that his keeper, Meurig, calls the Bwystfil were very good, superior to my first attempt. There is room for improvement when I come to version three – I would choose less disfigurement next time, more subtle pains to warp the mind. Perhaps then a new one wouldn't need locking up so much. The induced madness worked well, though a bit more stability and reliability would be good. I was very proud of the created ferociousness and cruelty; also the immunity to pain; and of the Pavlovian conditioning with stop words to prevent him ever turning on his Master.

"Overall? Six out of ten."

Chris said, "I know Meurig. Hunter in the woods."

"Yes. I doubt if you know the Bwystfil though. You wouldn't be here if you had met my red-coated pet."

"I'm glad I never met the guy," said Chris. Revealing what had happened at the lighthouse would only make Lord John more wary of him.

"Indeed.

"My masterstroke, the second advantage I had, was enhancing Turning by investing heavily in biotech that let me expand on Gittinger's work. Small labs always seem eager for money, and it gives access to many experimental drugs and chemicals that I can incorporate into the rites held at the chapel. There are so many to play with, so many effects, from the emotional joys of fear, anger, and depression, to the physical consequences of pain, and visual or auditory hallucinations. The compounds are often unstable, but that is half of the fun, investigating – recording – modifying. Even the failures are valuable.

"Ah, failures.

"Sometimes the failures break down physically, in hundreds of ways that all make them useless. Sometimes it is mental. That was why new innovations are tested on guests to the island, such as the so-called man in the cage over there. It wouldn't do to waste islanders, my only finite resource."

Chris couldn't help himself. He was feeling sicker the more Lord John spoke. "So you tortured the guy in there? Killed people – for what? To make some fucking zombies?"

Lord John looked at him disdainfully. "Now you are showing your ignorance, Chris. There are no supernatural powers involved with Turning – just a lifetime of perfected conditioning and xenophobia that can unleash aggression with no social control. Only my control."

"But why, for fuck's sake? To what end?"

"Look, if it bothers you, imagine it is good for them. Good for getting rid of dead wood. Good for improving science. Good for the possibilities in the future. Good for the islanders. Good for backwards people like the Welsh to have a master who can guide them."

"I'm sure they see it that way too," Chris growled.

"I'm glad we have a concord."

"We haven't. I was being sarcastic."

"I know. You haven't got the mental capacity for irony."

"I understand words like 'waste', and 'pointless', and 'talking crap'."

"Waste? Once the system is perfected it becomes a *commodity*. Tradeable. Many would buy it. On both sides of the law."

"So all this is for *money*?"

"No. It is for much more than that. Power and fun, too. And a new life, away from here, taking things further in advanced facilities. We can get so far."

"We?"

"Great Uncle Philip and – no, that's not right. He's dead." Lord John looked lost for a second.

"You're totally ... absolutely ... straitjacket-wearing mad."

At that Lord John flinched; then he strode over, snatched up the electric prod, and thrust it against Chris's chest. The pain and heat shot through him but he couldn't escape, couldn't back away as everything went white and every muscle fought against itself – only for a couple of seconds, but when the pain stopped and his body sank, spent, he felt exhausted. He could taste blood in his mouth; damn tongue had got in the way.

"I had thought we were getting along well, Chris. What have you got to say for yourself now?"

Chris painfully raised his head to look Lord John in the eye. "Untie my hands and I'll show you what mental capacity I've got."

Lord John gazed back coldly. "I think that – even now – I underestimate you."

"A lot of people do."

"The lighthouse, for example. You threw a real spanner in the works there."

"It was a wrench."

"Don't be facetious. You broke a pattern that had gone on for a long time."

Chris nodded. "I'll break more than that if I get the chance."

Lord John sighed, then calmly replaced the hand device, and picked up a scalpel. It glinted cruelly with reflected artificial light. "You seem so fearless, but no-one is, not really. We all have things we fear," he said softly. He moved the curved cutting edge of the scalpel to the flesh just below Chris's right eye, and held the cold steel there, puckering the skin. "In a second I could slice a chunk of your face off, or take out an eye. Do you want to say anything to me now, Chris? Do you?"

Chris forced his mouth to stay closed, despite an urge to say any of the hundred things in his head. He just glared back. Lord John seemed pleased. He lowered the scalpel and laughed.

"You are so strong. I don't want to do that really, it was a mistake I made with the second Bwystfil. No, I will break you but leave your looks, such as they are. You'll be more use as a puppet then. Third generation. Still, it is a good tool in my arsenal. I am amazed at how deforming someone's face can affect their personality so much. The simple threat of real disfigurement and people will do anything – it even shut you up."

He let the scalpel drop back onto the tray with a clang, to Chris's relief.

"You wouldn't believe the things people promise, just to evade the knife. *Please don't cut me any more, Mister! I'll be good*," Lord John imitated in what he clearly thought was a comedy voice. "Yet once you've done some slicing or burning on a face – if you do *enough* – they won't leave! I've tested it many times. Him over there – I left his door open, but he didn't escape. Didn't even try to leave his cage once his face had gone wrong.

"But that's the thing. I won't cut you in obvious places. I'm too careful now about my plans. I'm sensible, you see, and that is my final advantage over my ancestors. Whereas they were mostly mad, I – Lord John – am a genius. My intelligence could unleash the brutality in almost anyone. My head is screwed on right. Unlike poor Megan's."

The Switch

"The beginning of wisdom is to call things by their right names." – Chinese proverb

Lord John had left the room, "To fetch some tools I will need before we get started." Chris struggled against his straps. His hands tingled as feeling returned; still mostly useless, but he kept moving them to speed their return to life. If he were to do anything, he'd need them.

He tried sliding his body down in the seat, but the chest strap just caught under his armpits. With his wrists fastened he couldn't wriggle up and through the chest strap either.

Things couldn't get much worse.

Megan's head had been taken away by the Lord, which was a small mercy: Chris didn't have to deal with her dead, one-eyed gaze.

Pain throbbed in his leg from the cut, another discomfort vying for attention along with the headache, dizziness, hunger and still-present thirst. "Join the club," Chris muttered to his body. "Fucking traitor, I could do with some support, not more shit."

"I ... can't help ... much," came from the cage behind him, in swallowed consonants that made the hairs on the back of his neck rise. "But ... the drugs ... wearing off now." Then a groan.

Chris turned as much as he could. "Hey, you okay, man? I thought you'd died."

"He won't ... let me ... die." The deformed man sobbed.

"While there's life there's hope, mate. My name's Chris, and I'm fucking glad to have someone sane to talk to."

"My name ... used to be ... Tom. Tom ... Stanley." Another wrenching sob. "But cycled to island ... he caught me ... did ...*this* ... to me ... Now what am I? He messes ... with your mind and ... body."

"I gathered that. The fucker's mad." Chris tried to look Tom in the eye, but it was hard. Partly because of the twisted angle, but mostly because looking at Tom's face made him sick – the way the skin was bubbled and artificial-looking. But he didn't want to let his disgust show. He needed all the help he could get.

"You ... you will be next," sobbed Tom, who then wiped his face with the arm that ended in a stump, stretching the pink skin in a nauseating way. "I feel ... sorry ... for you."

"He can do his worst," said Chris defiantly, though he felt not one speck of the confidence of his words.

"He will ... break ... you. Like me. I'm ... awake now ... but maybe drugs ... again. Not much ... time. The drugs ... and videos ... and the stuff he does in your head ... electric shocks and ... torture. It's ... worse than you can ... imagine." Tom seemed to have trouble breathing too. Dirty, deformed, drugged, body parts missing, naked apart from the grubby T-shirt. Chris could fully believe how bad things would be.

"Can you ... do it?"

"Do what?" asked Chris.

"Kill him? Like you .... said ... to him."

Chris thought it over. But only for a second. "If I get the chance."

"Maybe ... I can help. And you ... then ... help me. I just ... just want to ... get somewhere *safe* ... get *better*."

"I'll do my best, mate. You can count on that. If you can help me at all then I'll owe you me fuckin' life."

"Then ... now is your ... only chance. If you go ... in this cage ... no way out. *Ever*. Chains ... in here." Tom pointed at the narrow length padlocked round his ankle. It ran to a hoop on the wall. "And he ... always ... uses drugs if ... he takes you ... out for other tortures. Always weak ... ill and ... sick ... confused. Don't get put ... in here."

"How can you help though? I've got to –"

But Tom turned, and with his remaining hand reached behind a pair of dirty bowls bolted to the wall – *for food and water*, Chris realised with a shiver. Something scratched, crunched grit-tily. Tom shuffled to the edge of his cage and put his good arm through the bars, reaching as far as he could. A shiny item glinted in his dirty fingers.

"Bit of glass ... sharp," gulped Tom. Chris wondered if his throat and tongue were swollen or deformed too, which would explain the problem speaking. He wished he hadn't realised that: the image was too distressing. "One torture ... he gave me ... a big mirror. After ... after doing this to my face! I smashed it. He ... punished ... me. This bit ... he missed, slid behind wires ... there. For ages I ... could see it ... worried he would ... see it too ... when in cage. But did ... didn't. One day ... left cage ... open ... chain undone. I *knew* it was ... a trap. But I got ... glass, then back in ... cage. Expected him ... to know. But didn't. Hid it ... not had use yet. A backup ... scared ... use it myself ... on me ... keep thinkin' of it ... Maybe you ... use it ... then take me ...*away* ... or kill me."

Tom started crying again, almost broken but still a man behind the mask.

At first Chris's hopes were dashed – what use was a fucking shard of glass? But then he had an idea. He had to get the shard into his hand, though. "Can you pass it to me?" he asked Tom.

"Only ... only slide it on floor."

"I need to be able to put my foot on it. Shit – this is only one shot, Tom. If I can't get it then the cunt will see what we were doing. We're both fucked then."

"Yes."

Tom put his hand on the floor, resting the shard there. Luckily the floor was flat concrete. If Tom aimed it right the shard would slide.

"Do you think he's watching? On the camera?"

"Don't know. Can't. Just ... hope."

Chris nodded. It wasn't like he had a Plan B.

Tom moved the shard back and forth, estimating the distance he needed to slide it to get near Chris's legs, back and forth, back and forth. Chris could do nothing to help, his palms sweating and gaze fixed hypnotically on the shard despite the pain in his neck from being so twisted. *Come on mate, you can do it.* Tom moved his wrist again, let go, the piece of glass skidded ... and it stopped short of Chris's chair, in a position he had no chance of reaching.

"Shit!" he cursed through gritted teeth. "Shit shit shit shit shit shit shit!"

Tom gazed at the splinter of glass, then lay on his side and reached through with his good arm, stretching as much as he could, his fingertips just short of the edge of it. The chain round his ankle pulled taut. Chris held his breath, willing Tom on, and Tom forced his shoulder tighter against the bars and grunted, stretching further, almost touching it ... Chris tried not to hope. The disappointment would be too great.

A noise somewhere outside, a door perhaps.

Tom groaned and stretched, then with a last effort shoved just enough to connect with the edge of the shard and it slid another few feet. Now it was well out of reach of Tom, who retracted his arm and knelt by the bars, watching intensely.

Maybe ...

Chris slipped as low as he could in the seat again, reached his foot back and to the side, the top of his foot scraping the ground, and his body badly twisted as he attempted to watch what he was doing. The chair was solid, bolted to the floor, but if he could stretch enough then there was a chance. He had to get his toes to the glinting splinter. A noise outside the door but he couldn't think of that, just had to stretch out – and amazingly his toenails were near it. Tom was rocking back and forth, moaning, but Chris focussed on this one chance. If he knocked it too soon it would slide further away, so despite the pain he lifted his foot *like a fucking yoga teacher, me, fuck yeah,* toes down then, in contact with the glass, edging it towards the chair, praying it wouldn't catch ...

The heavy metal door began to creak

pull, pull closer

and open as Lord John pushed

and suddenly it was moving, now under the chair as he straightened himself up

and walked into the room and noticed Chris readjusting his body after an apparently obvious – and futile – attempt to get out of the straps; he saw Chris put his feet flat on the floor.

But he didn't see what was underneath Chris's sole.

"I've been busy next door," said Lord John, removing a hypodermic syringe from his pocket. There was a blue plastic cap over the needle. "See this, Chris? See the lovely golden liquid inside? Fatal to humans in this dose. A truly lethal injection. A final solution to so many problems."

Chris imagined some of the problems he could solve with the needle.

"But first, a show. The thing in the cage over there is a failure. But even my failures are a partial success, beyond most people's imagined achievements. I work with control words, you see – words really can be mightier than the sword when I utter them. Well, as long as they are implanted under drugged suggestion. The puppet doesn't even realise the controls are there, but they exist nonetheless – a mostly unnecessary failsafe of which I am particularly pleased. Nothing to say to that? All right, I will proceed. Chris, you may wish to watch the cage-thing."

Chris turned to look at Tom, who had ceased his agitated swaying.

"Right, cage-thing, stand up and show us your little willy," ordered Lord John.

Tom shook his over-large head slowly, breath shortening.

"Go on. Or it will be the worse for you."

"Leave him alone!" snapped Chris.

"Presently. See how he refuses? Have you noted that? Right."

Lord John leaned towards the cage and muttered something Chris couldn't catch.

"*Now* stand and show us your willy."

Tom was shaking, his breath disturbed again. If anything, his face got redder as he slowly stood, while still shaking his head. He cried aloud as his hand lifted his dirty T-shirt to reveal something that wasn't right –

Chris turned away quickly. "For Christ's sake leave him alone!"

Lord John chuckled. "He doesn't want to do it – but he obeys anyway! Oh, Chris, I can't make you turn and look – not yet – but you know it is amazing. You in the cage, stop blubbering like a cry-baby. We've seen it. Now take this and inject it in your arm, depress the plunger all the way, then put the syringe back through the bars. Then die. Become the ultimate no-one."

"No!" Chris twisted to see Lord John holding out the loaded needle. Sobbing, Tom reached and took it. "Don't do it, Tom! Ignore the bastard, he can't make you do anything!"

Lord John's punchably smug smile seemed wide enough to split his face. "You know his name? Mmm," he said, thoughtfully. "Won't help though."

Tom held the syringe in his one hand and moved it with a nervous inevitability towards the stump where his other hand had been. The needle glinted, the reflection disappearing as the point slid under skin. Lord John could barely contain his excitement and seemed to be on the verge of jumping up and down and clapping his hands, but even though Chris shouted at Tom until his voice was hoarse Tom still pushed the plunger, forcing the liquid into his bloodstream, and Chris wasn't even sure how much was motivated by these so-called control words, and how much was his own wish to end the pain and degradation and endless horror of being subjected to the sadist nearby. Once the syringe was empty he pushed it meekly back through the bars and slumped against the rear wall, shaking. Chris turned away, not wanting to see the rest; not wanting to see whatever was getting Lord John so excited.

"Suit yourself," said Lord John gaily, "but you will miss the best bits!"

How long? How long had Chris been here in this room of suffering? An hour? Twelve hours? He couldn't tell, but he felt like a lifetime of horror had been compressed into the time.

For the next ten minutes, while Lord John occasionally giggled, Chris tried to ignore the pained noises from the cage and focus on the reassuring glass beneath his foot, a chance without which he would have no hope at all – a single chance to do something.

Eventually there was a sad sigh from Lord John, followed by the sound of unlocking and a rattle of metal chain. Then grunting.

Chris looked round briefly to see Lord John struggling to pull Tom out of the cage. Arms interlocked under Tom's armpits, Tom's back against the stained lab coat, Lord John slowly dragged his corpse out of the cage, panting. "I wish I already had you trained," he said to Chris, the humour forced from his face by exertion now, "then you could do this." Tom's head was flopped against Lord John's chest. "Got to ... get the cage free, Chris. Free ... for you," Lord John said between gasps as he dragged Tom's body across the floor. "You'll need to be in it ... for a few months ... while I work on you. This thing ... was in there for two. Oh, Chris!" he said as he neared the metal door leading out of the room – the door of escape. "I'll dump the body, then we'll be alone. Just you and me. For a long time."

By the time Lord John had dragged the body through the secret passage and into the coal room he felt exhausted. He let it flop to the floor and kicked it twice in frustration before closing the entrance to his "private research rooms", as he referred to them.

Manual labour was so demeaning.

But tidiness was a large part of his personality – he would not be able to take pleasure in his studies unless he tidied this failure away somewhere first. He would drag it out into the rear garden, to the family tomb. He could leave it there for now, and get a villager to dig a grave for it tomorrow. That was assuming he could find any villagers – there had still been no answer when he had tried the radio shortly before preparing the lethal injection. The last dose of elixir he'd given them at the special communion was larger than normal, so most were probably semi-conscious or sleeping it off. Only a few would have had an adverse reaction and died.

Lord John dragged the carcass again, across the gritty floor towards the stone steps out of the cellar. This part was always the most trying. One day he really would have to get some concrete taken up, so he could have an earth floor in one room down here. Then he could have a much more efficient workflow: into one room for research, and eventually under the earth in another. No need to drag bodies around like this.

He thought about all the fun to come, and that cheered him up and gave him a burst of energy. He dragged the corpse up the stairs by its ankles, heedless of its head cracking against the stone. His thoughts were so wrapped up in plans for Chris.

Things were already off to a good start. Megan would have had value for experimenting, but he had sacrificed her despite that, to take away Chris's hope and instil fear. Calculations suggested it would be a workable trade-off to open proceedings with a major blow like that.

He thought he would begin by sedating Chris and moving him into the cage. Then he could get started on the A-Treatment: knockout doses of Sodium Pentothal; followed by Benzedrine every so often to keep Chris semi-conscious and in a state where he would be open to suggestion, especially when other narcotics were brought into the mix.

His next plans were to work on ten-minute brainwashing scenarios based around the perception of rape. He suspected Chris would react strongly to those. They would aid trauma reconditioning, and, if combined with electric shock therapy, could help to promote memory loss which would open up other inroads into Chris's psyche. Depression and emotional instability would soon follow.

Oh, it was going to be so much fun! And he could get started so soon!

"*Be' sy'n bod arnat ti*?" ["What's the matter with you?"] asked Brân Ddu, squatting down to the snotty little boy's level.

"*'Nhad. Mae o'n sal. Dydy o ddim yn neis. Darodd o fi.*" ["My dad. He's sick. He isn't nice. He hit me."] The boy wiped his nose on the back of a coat sleeve, adding a glistening line to the mucoid crust already there. His thick, grey double-breasted coat was too big for him.

Keith too, Brân Ddu thought. What *happened* last night? What was Lord John up to?

"*Gwranda, dos i'r 'sgubor. Cuddia 'no am 'chydig. Fyddi di'n iawn.*" ["Listen, go to the barn. Hide there for a while. You'll be okay."]

The boy nodded, sniffing, and she ran her hand through his thick hair, ruffling it.

"*Paid â phoeni, bach.*" ["Don't worry, little one."]

The boy looked behind her, his eyes widening at the same time as she heard the creak of the cottage door.

"'*Nhad i!*" ["My dad!"] yelled the boy.

"*Dos!*" ["Go!"] replied Brân Ddu. The boy ran off on his stumpy legs, wellies splashing through the mud. She stood and turned in one movement to face the boy's father. Keith seemed drunk, and staggered towards her, eyes bloodshot.

"*Be' ydy o?*" ["What is it?"] she asked, backing away.

He didn't answer.

"*Arhosa*, Keith." ["Stop."] She held up her palm to reinforce the gesture, but he grabbed her arm and yanked her off balance, his other hand snatching a handful of her hair. He stank, and a string of saliva hung from his lip as he growled.

Brân Ddu struggled, furious at being touched by a man without permission, but his grip was as strong as if his hands had locked into the claws of rigor mortis. She scratched and kicked at him and tried to free the hair he was tugging on. Keith ignored her commands and wrestled her partway down the lane, while she struggled to remain on her feet. Her head was lowered by his grip in her hair, but she looked at the ground for anything that she could use as a weapon. They were alongside a knee-high wall topped with irregular slabs of slate that defined the garden of the next cottage, so she stepped over it and lurched back. He held on to her and was tripped by the barrier, then fell forwards, losing his grip and sprawling in the dirt. She kicked him once in the head and ran; she was already a good distance away before he got shakily to his feet and pushed through the bushes in pursuit.

She held on to her anger. Things had gone too far. First she would go to the chapel, for the protection she needed; then she would go to Lord John's mansion.

She was Brân Ddu, and she wanted answers.

Even though she panted from running, her teeth were bared in a grin. Because after finding answers, she could get revenge for her humiliation last night.

Time was precious and Chris was impatient, but he still waited until the noise of Lord John's struggling faded away – just to be sure he wasn't going to come back suddenly and catch him.

He had to get free before Lord John returned. If he was shackled in the cage, like Tom, he would be a goner. He had to cut loose now or never, despite the wasted state he was in, and despite the risk that Lord John might be watching on the camera.

Each wrist was tied separately and firmly to the heavy chair, with old, worn leather straps.

The shard was under his right foot. He slid it forward, so that when he craned his head he could just see it over his knees, despite the chest strap. Then he moved a foot to either side. Using his right big toe he gently pushed the glass to the left. By keeping his left sole on the floor he was able – after a few attempts – to raise the shard onto its edge, and it remained leaning on his left ankle. He made a gap between the big toe and the next toe on his right foot, and carefully manoeuvred his feet so the edge of the shard was between those toes. Then he curved those toes and closed them. He was able to lift his foot, and the shard lifted with it, held between his toes.

He knew he couldn't hold it there for long, and had been lucky to get this far without any mistakes.

Now he had, somehow, to get it to his hand.

He tried bending his right leg back at the knee, and to the side of the chair, but there was no way he could get the glass up to his right hand. Even as he attempted to, the shard slipped and he quickly put his foot back down, feeling the glass cut between his toes. But he still had it, and so moved everything forwards again.

It had to be his left then.

Knee bent at ninety degrees, he tried to raise his foot up to his left hand. However, he was nowhere near flexible enough to do it that way. He rested his leg and thought.

Next he tried the motion again, but this time he extended his left leg and rested his right foot on his left shin. From there he was able to start sliding his heel up the shin until it reached his knee and, by carefully wiggling his left leg, he eventually manoeuvred his foot above the knee. Thank God he was barefoot, this would have been impossible otherwise –

Then the glass slipped and fell to the floor with a clink.

Blinking back tears of frustration, Chris cursed under his breath; but at least the shard hadn't smashed into smaller – useless – pieces.

Be positive Chris. You know what to do. Just do it again – and don't drop it this time.

Oh, and hurry up too, you tosser.

He began once more, but this time he kept the toes of his right foot curved to better keep hold of the glass, though it was tiring the muscles and he couldn't keep them like that for long. It would be so easy to drop the glass again ...

Once he had the foot on the knee he continued to bend that leg. Carefully. By keeping his left heel on the floor but sliding it closer, it raised his left knee – painfully opening his right hip in a way he hadn't experienced before.

It looked so easy when he had seen women doing this. What was it, a half-lotus or something?

At this point he seemed to be stuck. His fingertips could almost touch the heel of his right foot. But they were still inches from his toes and the shard of glass.

Time was passing.

He would just have to keep going.

So began the grunting and straining as he alternately straightened, then bent, his left leg while trying to edge his right foot further up his thigh towards his left hand. It was agony. Sweat broke out on his forehead. The tension was unbearable as with every movement he feared dropping the shard. He wiggled his hips back as far as he could in the chair, which took his foot nearer again to his hand. He kept his toes curled in and, despite the pain, he curled them more, extending the sliver of glass nearer to his reaching fingertips. The two came into contact.

Just.

He gingerly pinched the sliver between his forefinger and index finger; relaxed his toes so the glass was now only held between the two digits; then straightened his left leg, letting his foot slip to the floor and relaxing the strain in his limb and crotch.

He ignored the thought that he might never walk again after that, and carefully lay the shard on the arm of the chair in front of his left hand.

Time was passing. But he had to get more feeling in his hand first. So he wiggled his fingers and rotated his wrist as much as the strap allowed. He then cautiously moved the shard around with his fingertips, into a position where he could hold it like a pen. By holding it near the end he was able to bend his wrist so that one part of the shard came into contact with the strap.

This would not be pretty, but he might already be nearly out of time, so if he cut skin (as he knew was inevitable) then so be it.

With a tight grip he started to saw away. It was uncomfortable and impractical, moving his hand back and forth, but he was thankful that the movement would stop his fingers from going numb. He was on the final stretch now, just had to hope the edge of the glass stayed sharp and helped cut through the tough leather.

He kept catching his wrist but he ignored that, speed was more important. He could imagine Lord John returning from wherever he had taken Tom at any second and – after all this effort – he couldn't bear the thought of being discovered before he had achieved anything. The thought was a killer, so he sawed on with renewed intention.

Too hard. A crack as the glass broke and a small piece tinkled to the floor. Not now! *Not now!* Chris squeezed his eyes hard closed, counted to three, then inspected the damage.

And let out the breath he'd been holding.

Luckily the jagged edge resembled a serrated knife, and as he continued the sawing motion he found it was even more effective. There was a definite furrow where the glass was cutting in, which helped reduce the amount of his skin he was slicing, but the blood was getting in the way.

"Always the small cuts that bleed the most," he muttered, wishing he could rest the hand as he experienced the first twinges of cramp.

Was that a noise somewhere above?

He sawed with revived ferocity, fraying toughened dead skin and soft living skin alike, listening for any sound beyond this room.

Yes: definite movement in the house.

But he wasn't even halfway through the leather, it wasn't fucking fair!

Now he heard something like a door nearby. There were footsteps coming closer.

As he sawed he estimated how much he had cut through; how tough the leather was; how strong *he* was.

It would have to do.

The door before him creaked open. Chris rested his wrist against the arm of the chair, shard beneath it, hoping the blood wasn't too obvious, or that if Lord John saw it he would just assume it was from struggling to escape.

"Hello, Chris," said the Lord, smiling beatifically and withdrawing another syringe from his labcoat pocket. "Are you ready to move into your new home?"

Brân Ddu tried to control her heart, which beat like the constant pattering raindrops. She glanced round – no-one had followed her to Lord John's mansion. She hammered on the front door's iron knocker again, but the booming echo was as the crash of waves against cliffs, and left her feeling alone and small.

It was only a short time ago that she had been forced to run from one of her own brethren. Normally the man was respectful and possibly even in awe of her, yet today he had grabbed and drooled like a monster. Things were a mess and she needed the key piece that would help to solve the puzzle.

She opened the heavy door, knowing it wouldn't be locked – only strangers who'd come from the mainland locked doors on Ynys Diawl. And so she walked into Plas Dof's entrance hall, quietly closing the door behind her after one more glance to check she wasn't being followed.

She sensed no living vibrations.

A large and delicately carved clock ticked by the umbrella stand. One of many clocks in Plas Dof. It was as if the Ynyr Fychans were obsessed with time, with measuring things out. She despised that. The more things were measured the smaller they seemed. Only surrendering to the bliss of a day, embracing what it brought without question, could lead to peace and prevent a day shooting by in the blink of an eye. The Ynyr Fychans weren't like her. This was something she had suspected before, but now – just from staring at their clock – the certainty gripped her even more strongly.

Part of her felt as if she should hurry. Seek out Lord John's hateful face. Find answers. But another part of her was like the hushed voice she sometimes heard in dreams, or from the relic. A calming voice. It seemed to whisper that she would find the answers she sought, there was no need to hurry, that nothing could be changed yet, and so she should not waste her energy swimming against the tide. She should relax into the flow until the tide turned, and have faith that she would reach the shore safely.

She rested her hand on the large, lumpy object inside her cardigan. It was a true voice, akin to her voice.

On impulse she took the first door, into a reception room. She had been here often. The faded but exquisite material of the antique couch had held her light body. The paintings, the books, the cushions in the window seat – all these were known to her. There were no answers here.

She left through an irregular, narrow door, which was squeezed between the corner and a cabinet of antique glasses. A short and shadowed corridor with no windows faced her. Leaving the door behind her ajar so she could see, she ran her hand along the textured wallpaper, inhaling the musty smell, then chose the door that led to the book-lined study.

An intricately-carved black fireplace, brass reflection telescope on the deep window ledge, leather sofa, desk, and bureau whose wood was blackened by age – she knew this room too. It didn't feel like a *lair*. She suspected Lord John made that elsewhere in the house. But he used this room; his essence was imprinted in the soft leather of the seat behind the desk, and the selection of books which lay open on it. She glanced at them with distaste. She was sure they contained some truth, but once it was put into words in that way it became less than the experience; it changed the essence; it became false. Most books were for men, and foreigners from the mainland, not for people who would rather live life than read about it.

She shuffled through the items on the desk then moved to the drawers, rooting through them impatiently. One drawer was locked. She swept papers from the top of the desk until she found a sturdy steel paper knife and used it to prise open the drawer, which yielded with a dry splitting of aged wood. Money; old photographs of family, curled at the edges; keys; and some modern pictures of naked men and women in vulgar poses, artificial and polluting. Rubbish.

She went to the chestnut writing bureau. It wasn't locked, and contained nothing of interest. Fancy paper and envelopes and pens and inks and stamps and letters.

She bit back the spark of irritation and scanned the room. She was sure there was something here. Something that would be more revealing than the lies she would get when she confronted Lord John.

The bookcase. *How he loves his books.*

She examined it more carefully. One section was built against the wall with the entrance hall on the other side. Another section was built against the wall behind his desk. She did not know what room was beyond those stones.

She slid books around, looking behind them. Some she threw to the floor, examining shelves. Knots and old cracks were prodded. She knocked on the wood at the back. One back panel made a different sound to the others. The shelf in front was looser. She followed it along and found a fine line. A sister line ran up the back of the bookcase in the same spot. They touched.

She rattled the shelf again after throwing more books and a stone bookend to the floor, and when the shelf lifted slightly she could open a small section on a hidden hinge, revealing a square compartment about eighteen inches wide and twelve high. It was piled up with papers and hand-written books, which were obviously diaries when she flicked through a few. They were written in many hands and were of different ages – some were so old that the ink was fading. She selected the most recent-looking diary.

"Huh. *Yn Saesneg.*" ["In English."]

It was Lord John's writing.

She sat at the desk and started reading.

"What's that for?" asked Chris.

"To put you to sleep, my friend. You are hardly going to go peacefully, are you?"

"Maybe. If you ask me nicely."

"I am not *naive.*"

If he injects me then I'm done.

"No, you're not," said Chris with a pretend sigh. "But you are always so calm. How do you do that? How do you stay cool?"

"Breeding, I suppose – plus willpower."

"Yeah, willpower. I could show you willpower."

"Yes?"

"Yeah. It's a special trick I've got."

"What's your game?" asked Lord John suspiciously. "You're up to something."

"Kind of. I'm hoping if I let you in on a secret maybe you'll trust me a bit more."

"I don't think that's your game at all." Lord John's eyes were narrowed. Had he seen the small piece of glass on the floor?

"Let me whisper it to you," Chris said, trying to keep attention on himself. "Lean down here."

"You're practically transparent, Chris."

"You'll never see the secrets I have inside me unless I tell you now."

"Oh yes, I will. But enough. Time to end this panto."

Keep spinnin' the bullshit. Got to get him off balance. Got to stop him using the needle.

"Well, you said I surprise you. You said you like that. I want to show ya somethin'."

"And what might that be?"

"That zapper of yours. Do you reckon you can hurt me with it?"

"You know the answer to that already, Chris."

"No way! That was just a tickler before. I've felt more during a fuckin' orgasm. That was for pussies, surely?"

Lord John's hands twitched, but he said nothing.

Bite, you fucker.

"I reckon I can take it and spit it back out. Try me! I want it."

"There will be plenty of time for that later." Speaking curtly, and having apparently made a decision, Lord John stepped towards Chris, taking the plastic cap off the needle.

"Cunt!" Chris yelled. "You're a cunt and a coward, and I want you to zap me with your little toy so I can show you something you've never seen before! Don't be a fucking retard – *Johnnie.*"

The Lord stopped, looking surprised and unsure of what was going on. Apparently he didn't like that feeling. "I'm disappointed in you, Chris."

"Cunt!"

"What *is* your game?"

"Cunt pussy! Zap me and find out!"

"I thought you were going to play along –"

"Sad little fucker!"

"– and now all these obscenities –"

"You're a fuckin' loony, that's what, if you don't electrocute me right now! Tosser –"

"– it is so tiresome –"

Come on – you got angry before, do it once again, just for me – strip away the polite chit-chat shit and be what you really are.

"– pretending to be so cool when you're scared of me really, that's it, yeah! SCARED of me like a little shit –"

"Shut up."

"– old wasted wanker, can't fuck I bet, that's it, can't wank or fuck so you take it out on me –"

"Shut up, Chris."

"– you want me to shut up because the truth hurts: you're no man –"

"Shut up, yes I am –"

"Untie me and see who's the man then, you little cunting runt!"

Bite, you fucker, bite.

"You will be so sorry if you keep on with this –"

If this went wrong was he going to be any worse off than before? At the end of the day he was dead. He had to use his old trick: to overbalance the Lord, take his centre, turn the situation, provoke, press the right buttons, at the right times, and keep the pressure on.

"I'm not sorry for nothing, you shit-soft posh cunt!"

To bring him down he had to use the Lord's chosen weapons. Words.

But Chris's own words.

"I can take all you fucking throw at me, turd-bird arse-licker, you bat-winged bitch, do your worst! Let me show you what I am, what I *really* am!"

Chris was letting himself get worked up, spittle flying as he strained and yelled and dredged his mind for any inspiration. He knew he was nearly there, Lord John was fully tightened with anger, everything pulling up like a tornado and ready to lose control and fling it all back out –

"I can take it! Zap me! Cunt-runt baby-boy, midget big-head, old coot with no cock, you wanna see somethin' you've never seen before? You twat, oh yes, Lord Twattie! Twat, twat – don't like that, eh? Can't swear so you don't like me doing it? Fuck, arse, you mother-fucking shitbearding ras clart jam-rag –"

And Lord John flung the needle onto the trolley and snatched up the handheld electric shock device, and Chris grinned like a maniac and yelled that he wanted it, and Lord John thrust it against his chest and pressed the switch but Chris hardly noticed the pain in his worked-up adrenaline rush as he gritted his teeth and used every bit of energy to contract each muscle while being shocked, and with a snap the leather gave way to the over-strained muscles in Chris's left arm, fist tensed – Lord surprised for a second and stopping – Chris smashed Lord John's hand away, not expecting it to work but Lord John dropped the device while Chris grabbed his lab coat and yanked him forward – thank Christ he had come so close! – and headbutted him right on the nose with a real cruncher before flinging him back, off balance, to stagger into the metal door.

With no time to waste Chris used his left hand on the other strap, having already unfastened it many times in his head over the last few hours. Lord John was getting his wits about him and staggering across to the trolley as Chris undid the chest strap with trembling hands, thankful hands. Off the chair, he hit Lord John in the face before he could pick up the needle. Lord John fell, stunned.

He blinked twice as Chris knelt beside him, a look of incomprehension at the speed of events, the reversal. "No, you can't do this – I'm the Turner," he whined to Chris, blood running from one nostril and into his mouth.

"Stitch this," replied Chris, slamming a fist into his face. "You see, I got my own kind of turning – my way of turning a situation round." He hit him again with a pleasurable crack.

"It's what I did on you just now; what I did on that big red-coated motherfucker on the lighthouse; what I've done to many others that deserved it over the years. Thing is, my *name's* Turner, *and it has been all my life* – so I'm better at it than you. I'm Chris Turner. And you shouldn't have fucked with me."

Bailing Out

"You taught me language; and my profit on't is, I know how to curse." – Shakespeare, *The Tempest*

The rooms all looked so *fine* – such a contrast from her lonely and bare home. The gentlemen's and ladies' drawing rooms; the beautiful bar room, with a huge billiard table that hadn't been played on for years but still had all the balls set out for a game; every room stuffed with dusty antiques, faded art, old and noble sculptures.

Brân Ddu wanted to destroy them all. Smash every mirror and split everything which had stuffing.

Her anger was fuelled to crackling and spitting point by the diaries, hate growing as she realised it was all madness and lies; derision for her and the other islanders.

The diaries explained so much – why most people she had found today were unconscious, dead, or uncontrollably dangerous.

Yet nowhere was the one she sought.

He had to be here somewhere! She sensed it!

There was a reckoning to be had.

Chris edged his way through the mansion, his back sliding along the plaster wall, listening for any sound. But there was only one – the low groaning behind him.

"Shut the fuck up!" he hissed, yanking Lord John closer.

Lord John's face was a mess. Chris was sure he'd smashed some of his teeth in below the split lip, broken nose and swollen eyes. Even now he was surprised at his restraint.

It's the new me. Mr Self Control.

There he'd been, sat astride Lord John's chest, punching away, wrapping his hands around the scrawny throat to strangle the fucker – and then he stopped.

All his life he had acted on impulse; given in to the emotions of the moment.

And it had always got him into trouble.

He should have learnt to think by now, so that was what he did. A minute later, he dragged Lord John up. Chris realised that the Lord was his best chance of escape. If he was the head honcho then, as a hostage, he might persuade the villagers to back off if they ran into any. So for now he lived. At least until Chris got the truck to the edge of the island.

He entered the hall beneath a magnificent chandelier. Every shadowy doorway held potential danger, so he stayed on guard.

Chris had contemplated looking for food, water, possibly clothes and shoes, but he was so close to freedom he decided to take no risks. Discomfort wouldn't kill him. Hunger wouldn't kill him. The headaches and pain and cuts wouldn't kill him. He was so focussed on escape he didn't even nick any of the obviously expensive things in the house.

"Everything here's probably jinxed," he muttered to himself.

He checked his pocket. The pickup key had gone. He should have expected that. Lord John was barely conscious. No point in asking him for its location.

It didn't matter. He'd be happy to walk after being tied up for so long. Daylight flooded in through the stained glass windows in the hall and the ticking grandfather clock showed 4.23pm, so – unless he had been unconscious for more than a day – he must have been confined for six or seven hours.

So short a time.

Maybe that's what Hell is like.

Movement in the doorway to his left. He snatched the Lord forwards, put his arm around his thin neck in a position where he could snap it, or at least do serious damage. A fresh gobbet of blood dripped onto the labcoat, which was now smeared red right down the front.

A pale face emerged from the doorway, with an expression that changed from a frown to a look of surprise in a second.

"You?" Chris asked.

"You?" asked Anne Jenkyns.

She eyed him with a strange look which Chris couldn't define. He didn't like it. Then she recognised the face beneath the blood, and flinched. "You have the Lord!"

Lord John seemed to rouse, and realise who she was. “Mmph-grnr!” he tried to say. “Mph, ghjtuyt!”

But amongst the broken teeth and pain he couldn’t articulate much. After flinching when he first made a sound, Anne now strode forward more purposefully, one arm beneath her long black cardigan.

“Stop there!” Chris stepped back, keeping Lord John between himself and her. “Come any nearer and I’ll snap his neck. Then yours.”

She stopped. “You did this to him?” she asked.

“Yes. And there’s plenty more for anyone else who tries to stop me leaving.” He forced the sudden dizziness away – he had to appear strong.

“I won’t stop you leaving.” Her voice was soft, strongly accented and appealing.

“I know. No-one will.”

“No, Chris – you misunderstand. I’m *glad* you’re alive. I came here to kill *him* – and I found *you*.”

“How can I believe that?” Chris asked. “You’re all his ‘subjects’.”

“*Were*. But he’s gone too far, and now I know the truth about him. He’s a fake and an imposter and he’s been around here too long. The only reason I stopped when you said to was because *I* want to be the one who kills him.”

There was such an intensity in her voice – such a sick yearning – that Chris believed her. Lord John struggled feebly and tried to speak again, but ceased when Chris squeezed tighter.

“He can’t speak – he has no power,” said Anne, with wonderment.

"That's right. No power and precious few fuckin' teeth, I reckon."

She smiled at that.

"But I thought you died at the lighthouse? They all went there, fired up with whatever *he* had done to them – and he sent the Bwystfil too. How did you survive?"

"If that's the big guy in red, then I fought him."

"You fought the Bwystfil?" She seemed incredulous.

"Yes. I threw the fucker off the lighthouse and smashed him into the ground."

Lord John gazed up with a pained expression then, Chris noted with satisfaction.

"And you were unhurt?" Anne persisted.

"I wouldn't say that. I fell off too. Just that I'm lighter, and went over the cliff and into the sea."

"And you survived," she said softly, with awe.

"It didn't feel like it. But I guess I'm a good swimmer."

She stepped closer, eyes wide with a look of – almost *reverence* – and reached out to touch Chris's face. He flinched back.

"Look, Anne, this is nice, but I've got to go."

"Brân Ddu."

"What?"

"Brân Ddu. It is my name."

"I'll never understand you."

"I think you will."

Chris shrugged, started to drag Lord John past her, but she held out a hand.

"Leave him. He must die."

Lord John twitched, presumably in response to her demand, but he made no sound.

"I can't do that. I need him in case I run into anyone."

She laughed at that.

"In the state I have seen people in today, he would not help. There is little danger there. Obviously this pathetic creature overstepped the bounds – whatever concoction he used at the male-only ceremony yesterday was too strong. Whether he intended it or not, some are in deep sleep. Some are in death's sleep. Some are mindless. They are a danger perhaps, but he wouldn't help you there. In fact, he would just slow you down. Keep low and off the road and you will be fine."

"How can I trust you?"

The smile that crept along her features seemed elfin, inhuman, and somehow troubling. "I like you; I hate him. You can trust me. He has had so much power – this is my one chance to get rid of him. Now, while he can't speak or whimper his way out of it. I can't risk him ever speaking again. You – you cannot be harmed by me even if I wished it. I want him to die. I want things to be different from his ways. I am begging for him so I can kill him – and you can watch me do it, which is my final proof."

She removed her hand from beneath her cardigan. In it she held a large, toothed bone, which Chris assumed had come from a shark or whale or some scary fish like that. "I will kill him with this, right now."

Again her grin, which changed her features in a way which fascinated and repulsed Chris at once – so beautiful that it was alien, and frightful.

Chris looked from her face to Lord John's, and back again.

"You want him? Okay." Then to Lord John, "And you ... you've got it coming."

Chris shoved Lord John towards her and headed for the front door, his back to them both.

"You don't want to watch?" she asked, halting his soft tread. "Watch me kill him?"

He shook his head as he turned. "I've seen enough bloodshed. Just make sure you do it."

"What will you do?"

"Try to live a quiet life. Again."

"I would have helped you, Chris. If I'd got the opportunity. If I'd known what was going to happen."

"It wasn't me who needed help," he replied, fist clenching. "But thanks anyway. Oh, by the way ..."

"Yes?"

"You should burn this fuckin' house to the ground."

Near the front door was a stout steel-topped walking cane. Chris picked it up, patted the head against his palm to check its solidity, nodded with satisfaction, and slipped out into the misty daylight.

She watched him go, then turned to the shaking man before her. Lord John tried to speak again, but it was incomprehensible.

"Command me now, Lord!" she laughed, light dancing in her eyes as she raised the arm holding the bone. "Your power is gone, and you are pathetic."

Lord John watched the arc of her arm as it fell, before the end of the bone crushed into his forehead, splitting the skin and cracking the skull beneath, collapsing part of the brow into his eye. He crashed backwards against the black and white tiles, blood streaming down the left side of his face. He threw up his left arm to defend himself but she struck that, smashing his forearm so his arm dropped, and before he could struggle to raise it again she struck the top of his head, his scalp tearing on a jagged tooth which pulled back a flap of skin with hair attached. He tried to crawl away using his unbroken arm, groaning in pain, but with an atavistic grin she raised the bone in both hands now and rained blows down with all her might on his spine and the back of his head. Soon the hall resounded with bruising thuds. The thumps changed to wet cracks as Lord John's skull caved in. Fluid and brain tissue splashed with each connection on the downswing, then flew through the air with every upswing of the bone, splattering on the ancestral paintings so the watching faces seemed to cry blood.

She staggered backward, out of breath but with an exultant shine in her eyes, her face paler than ever against the gore that had speckled it. A piece of brain fell wetly from the sleeve of her cardigan onto the floor.

"*Y mochyn! Nid Anne! Byth eto. Brân Ddu ydw i! Brân Ddu, ac rwyt ti wedi cael dy ladd! Crachen! Ti yw'r ffŵl! Yr hyn nad yw'n gynhenid ddylid ei daflu allan. Nid brodor wyt ti, y lleuen!*" ["You pig! Not Anne! Not ever again. Brân Ddu I am! Brân Ddu, and you've been killed! Scab! You are the fool! That which is not native should be cast out. And you are not native, louse!"] Her eyes gleamed, spittle flew from her lips in rage – then she rapidly calmed, tossing the blood-soaked bone casually onto the corpse before her.

She strode over to the front door and looked out, but Chris had already melted away from her eager eyes. Gone as if he had never been.

"*Cwymp fel 'na ... cymaint o gwymp i ddyn ... ei daflu o'r golau lawr i'r ddaear i ddechrau gwrthryfel. Mae patrymau i'w fywyd nad ydy o'n ei gweld, hyd yn oed. Ella'i fod o eisiau bywyd tawel, ond ella nad hynny ydy'i ffawd.*" ["A fall like that ... such a fall for a man ... cast out from the light and down to the earth to begin a rebellion. There are patterns in his life the man can't even see. He may want a quiet life, but that may not be his fate."]

She felt sure they would meet again. And until then she could organise and rebuild. Heal those that could be healed. They would all obey her now. She would see to it.

Having no strength left to run, Chris used all the cover he could as he moved west across the island, beneath a grey Welsh drizzle. Some of the trees, festooned with pale green lichens like ghostly webs, sabotaged stealth where the brittle fallen branches crackled underfoot. Chris edged from tree to tree, and hid behind moss-patched rocks and boulders, always peering carefully over the top before moving on. He saw no-one.

A breeze goosebumped his skin as dusk came on. He dared to hope. For despite the wind and spitting rain, things felt – well, spent.

The water level between Ynys Diawl and Anglesey seemed lower. He continued west. Two seagulls screeched overhead, then flew away. When he neared the sandbar he spent nearly half an hour under a bush, watching the road in both directions, looking for signs of an ambush. He saw no-one.

So he half-ran, half-loped to where the road ended and the sandbar began. It was there, still under water but starting to re-form, and it looked as if the water would only be waist deep at the deepest point. Although the water was fast flowing it wouldn't stop him now – he could ford it. And then head cross-country to a *big* town, not a village. He would hide when cars went past. Just in case.

There was a whine nearby. It came from the bushes.

He was tempted to ignore it, make the crossing now before anyone came.

The whine again. Whimpers.

He limped over to the bushes, parting them cautiously.

It was the black Labrador. The one he had sometimes seen the policeman walking. The one he had seen Megan hugging in the pub. It was lying down, head on its forepaws, its lead caught in the spiny branches.

He reached in and untangled it. The dog looked up at him, the crescent whites of its eyes showing. It gave a solitary despondent wag of its tail.

Chris unclipped its lead and threw it away.

"Go, dog," he said. "Your master is dead. Today they all are. Go."

It gave a feeble wag and shivered.

He turned and limped back towards the sandbar. Leaves rustled behind him. When he looked back at the dog, it lay on its side, legs open, tail curved between its back legs in a gesture of submission.

He squatted next to it and examined the medallion on its collar.

"Spotty, eh? What a daft name."

The dog thumped its tail.

"I suppose it's been a hard time for you too, huh?"

Another wag.

If Megan had lived ...

He had let her down.

He could do one thing right, though. One thing.

He held out his hand. The dog licked it.

"Come on, dog. Everybody needs somebody."

Time And Place Unknown

Chris jerked upright with an intake of cold air, the sheet sticking to his damp, bare chest. A quick glance around reassured him that all the shapes in the darkness were familiar ones.

He scanned the room a second time anyway.

A murmur next to him, but she was still asleep. Good.

He had thought a noise had woken him – an engine turning off, or a car door slamming – the kind of noises that got his attention now that he lived beyond the beaten track, even though they'd been a constant backdrop in the city.

Perhaps he'd just dreamt it, he told himself.

He edged out from under the sheet, careful not to disturb the naked body beside him. She mumbled incoherently and rested her arm across the space he'd vacated, then seemed to settle into sleep again. He made sure she was covered properly, preventing the warmth from escaping from under the thick bedding. When her breathing was deep enough he lifted his jeans off the back of a chair and quietly slipped out of the room into the dark hall, closing the door carefully so it didn't click.

The November air was chilly and he shivered, but it was better than sweaty nightmares. The house remained silent, undisturbed.

He slipped the jeans on over his muscled nakedness, and almost fell over when something wet caressed his hand in the dark, before he realised what it was.

"Shit. Don't do that, Spotty," he whispered. "Good dog though," he added apologetically, rubbing the dog's head.

No noises so far, and Spotty wasn't growling at anything. Still, he wouldn't get back to sleep unless he checked it out.

He opened the store cupboard at the top of the stairs. Below all the towels and stuff that smelt of soap he found the shelf with tennis rackets: next to them was a cricket bat. He took it and closed the cupboard, then crept down the stairs with the bat held loosely in one hand; only treading on the edge of the stairs next to the wall, because he knew they didn't creak there. The hall came into view and Spotty moved down past him, claws clattering on the tiles as, with better night vision than Chris, he trotted to the kitchen.

Before following him, Chris slipped into the front room. The window was closed, lace curtains undisturbed; everything in the right places. He glanced out of the window into the darkness, eyes more adjusted now, but the cold moonlight just revealed sculptures: frozen statues of trees beyond the colourless grass, the car a monument parked in front. No-one running from shadow to shadow. No pickup truck parked there with a bunch of burly, zombiefied murderers piling out, armed with rusty agricultural implements. Not a branch moving. He was satisfied. He rubbed his arms until the goose bumps faded.

His bare feet absorbed the iciness from the quarry-tiled floor. Spotty whined by the back door. A look through the window over the sink revealed nothing suspicious – only the unsettling stillness of a moon-graced garden, with fields beyond belonging to the farm further along the river.

He drew back the bolts and Spotty scrabbled eagerly outside, his motion setting off the external floodlights which bathed the rear of the house in yellow artificial light, overpowering the ethereality of the moon and restoring normality. The chilly breeze washing over Chris's chest was refreshing, drying the last of the sweat. He turned on the kitchen fluorescents and, after their clicking false starts, they buzzed into life.

Spotty seemed to be off in the bushes and not keen on coming straight back in. Chris sighed and got a drink of water.

"Damn dog."

After clunking the tumbler down onto the sturdy pine table he wandered into the hall and knelt by the bookcase. One shelf contained box files, variously labelled in a feminine hand as "Gas and Lec", "Bank and mortgage", "Council + odds". At the end of the shelf was one that said "Chris's Stuff". He pulled it out, flipped through the contents, then took an unlabelled cardboard-covered scrapbook to the kitchen. It was his special scrapbook.

He sat with his back to the open door, enjoying the challenge of trying to control his body and prevent it from shivering, then opened the scrapbook to the first page where the newspaper cuttings began. Each had source details scribbled above in biro.

Daily Star, September 14th

Police investigate disappearances on Stawl Island

Following an anonymous tip-off police have been investigating chilling accusations of foul play on Stawl Island, off the east coast of Anglesey.

The source alleged that people had been murdered as part of a spooky conspiracy during the night of the massive storm last week.

The freak storm snapped power lines and left plucky workers battling to restore services to stunned Brits.

The mystery source apparently contacted all national newspapers, and slammed the police for failing to protect people.

Alleged victims included a police officer and a school teacher. A spokesman for the police said they were investigating.

North Wales Chronicle, September 16th

Hotline on Stawl Island disappearances

A police hotline has been set up to gather information about anyone who has gone missing in connection with Stawl Island.

Police Chief Superintendent Peter Cartwright of North Wales Police said that any genuine disappearances would be investigated.

North Wales Chronicle, September 23rd

Hotline goes cold

A hotline set up to gather information about the allegations of disappearances on Stawl Island is to be closed.

Police Chief Superintendent Peter Cartwright of North Wales Police said that it had done its job, and all relevant information had been gathered.

An anonymous source in the police service implied that it had been shut down due to the large number of hoax disappearances being reported on it, wasting police time and resources.

"The investigations continue," said the Police Chief Superintendent. "The Stawl Island police force has co-operated fully, and any truth in the allegations will be brought to light. In order to help us, I would like to appeal to whoever started these rumours to come forward for questioning."

Bangor & Anglesey Mail, September 30th

Investigation closed

This paper gained an exclusive interview with Chief Superintendent Peter Cartwright yesterday. The Police chief said that the investigation into the alleged disappearances on Stawl Island has been closed after all possible lines of investigation had been followed.

Of the alleged disappearances he said: "We looked into it. There was no evidence of foul play. We suspect the claims were a hoax, probably the same people who made hoax calls during the big storm. A few people have been reported missing, but there is nothing to link most of them to Stawl Island. I feel very sorry for the families of anyone who has disappeared, but people disappear in many places, for many reasons."

Constable Emyr Huws was based on the island on the night in question, but the other officer stationed there is apparently one of the few genuine missing people. An anonymous police source told us the officer in question had been stationed on the island only for a short period, and it was suspected that he was suffering from depression following a traumatic event in his previous post, which may have led him to abandon his new position - a search for him continues.

Before ending the interview the Police Chief once again appealed to the anonymous person who started the rumours about mass murders, and who has tried to keep the story alive by continuing to send information to newspapers, to please desist and stop wasting police time.

The next page was a printout from a website.

October 6th

Press Release - Visit Wales/Croeso Cymru

Senior officials at Visit Wales are urging tourists to ignore the recent media coverage of alleged disappearances in Wales. Brian Llwyd, Deputy Chief Executive of Visit Wales told tourists and the media that a discredited anonymous source had recently been trying to run a campaign which cast doubt on the safety of tourists. "This person, whoever it is, obviously has some sort of grudge against Wales, and the tourist industry particularly in Anglesey," explained Mr Llwyd. "However, despite repeated calls for the person to come forward, they have not done so."

Mr Llwyd went on to say that Visit Wales took allegations of misconduct of tourist businesses, and threats to visitors, very seriously. Despite rigorous investigations by both the police and Visit Wales, no evidence was found to substantiate the wild rumours that were circulating in the tabloid press.

"I can only presume," concluded Mr Llwyd, "that the person is spreading these damaging rumours for malicious reasons. I wish to assure visitors that Wales remains an extremely safe place to visit. Our crime figures are the lowest in the whole of the UK, and tourists to our lovely country can expect to fall in love with majestic mountains, grand bays of golden sand, and dynamic and vibrant cities. Wales remains a safe, beautiful and welcoming place to visit during the coming half-term holiday."

Chris sighed and shook his head, turned to the next page. A cutting was neatly pasted into the centre of the sheet, with pride of place, and he grinned. A gust of wind blew through the trees in the garden, rustling their branches, as he read on.

Bangor & Anglesey Mail, October 13th
Missing Lord

Lord John ap Ynyr Fychan (54), of Stawl Island, has been reported as missing. A spokeswoman for the islanders, Anne Jenkyns (19), said that he had gone fishing off the coast of Anglesey, despite advice to the contrary because of the predicted bad weather. It is feared that his boat sank during a storm, though no trace of a wreck has yet been detected.

Lord John was the last of a long line of resident nobles on Stawl Island, going back to the fifteenth century when Lord Weston was granted the island and successfully stopped the piracy taking place in the area. From then on the waters and lands around Ynys Diawl were safe. In the eighteenth century the thirteenth Lord Weston changed the family name and became Lord Ynyr Fychan, perhaps to portray the Welshness the family felt after three hundred years ruling an island off Anglesey, and since then there had been an almost unbroken line of Ynyr Fychans as resident Lords of this small domain.

He has no heirs. If indeed he has perished in an unfortunate accident, then the passing of this noble man (well known for giving money to cancer and medical research charities) will mark the end of an era.

Chris flicked the page with his middle finger before turning over. He skimmed over the last few cuttings and printouts, only pausing at the two most recent.

Fortean Mysteries, October issue "Halloween Special"
Mass disappearance on Devil Island

Observant readers may remember a flurry of stories last year, concerning the claims that many people had disappeared while holidaying on Stawl Island, Wales. Then, just as suddenly, the story ended, with the main papers saying it was a hoax.

But was it a hoax? Many claim that things are not quite right on that remote stretch of rock.

Stawl Island is not named after a person, as many believe. It is so named because in Welsh it is called 'Ynys Diawl' - 'Devil Island'. [Stawl = corruption of '...s Diawl' - Ed.] It is no surprise that with a name such as that, the island has a long and sinister history. There are rumours of piracy (in the 16th and 17th centuries), murder, disappearances - and Satanism. The current chapel is Calvinistic Methodist, but tales of 12th century monks with dubious habits [! - Ed.] exist. The island has ominous legends, such as the ones which say that on moonlit nights the faces of the dead look out from the sea; or those about the 'Bwci Bach Llanfychan', the little red goblin that myth says haunts the island's woods.

Others have talked about the significance of numbers. To take just one example, the island is 171 hectares, 171 being a multiple of the occult number 9*; on the night of the storm the lighthouse was damaged, the beams sticking at 99° and 279° respectively - again, that number 9 keeps recurring. [*Discussed in the numerology article last month, 9 is the only number that can be multiplied by any other number, and the sum of the answer always leads back to 9. E.g. 9x7=63, 6+3=9. This sum applies to the cited numbers 171, 99, and 279 as well. - Ed.]

It is also claimed that Stawl Island lies across three ley lines known to be a magnet for extra-terrestrial activity.

Whatever you believe, and whatever the reason, the most disturbing story is this: the island's cliffs have proven to be a suicide and danger hotspot, and official records show a suspicious number of deaths with the verdict of 'misadventure'.

Could evil practices be going on there still?

paganwales.blog.org/articles/satwales.asp

Satanists in Wales

I'm branching out for this article (or bunch of ramblings, if Peon675 is to be believed!), but it is linked with Paganism and Wicca in some ways, and ties in with the bunch of links posted here.

It is interesting that Satanists have been accused of Ritual Abuse - especially back in the 1980s, when many sensational books were written by extremist evangelical Christian sects. Child abuse, torture and murder were described; it seemed that psychologists uncovered hidden memories, and a hysterical 'witch hunt' followed.

However, on later investigation, in a calmer frame of mind, most of the 'evidence' was found to be false. Any crimes committed were not by true Satanists, but by mentally disturbed or confused dabblers. It is a fact that most religiously motivated crimes committed in the US are actually committed by … Christians! Fundamentalist Christian hysteria about abortion clinics are just the tip of the iceberg.

There were claims that Satanists had been involved with murders on the Welsh island of Ynys Diawl, perhaps due to a misunderstanding about the name of the island: 'Diawl' means 'Devil', but the name probably comes from the murky past when the island was a suspected base for piracy. The idea that a group of Satanists who were intent on evil deeds would want to be so overt as to name the island after themselves is stupid. "Here we are!" Yeah, right.

It was also claimed that the so-called 'disappearances' took place during some sort of high holiday for Satanists - talk of it being the ninth day of the ninth month, 9/9, which (inverted) gives us 616: the 'Number of the Beast' according to many sources. (NOT 666 - blame the film series 'The Omen' for that misconception). It is nonsense because true Satanists don't celebrate particular dates (apart from the Solstices and Equinoxes - and maybe birthdays). The fact that the date was characterised by bad weather in Wales last year seemed to be further evidence to conspiracy theorists. However `bad weather in Wales in September is not supernaturally strange! A true Cymro wouldn't bat an eyelid. Basically, there isn't much evidence that anything went on at Stawl Island anyway, and certainly none that Satanists were involved.`

Since Chris had got off the island he'd been keeping an eye on the papers and news – but there had been no more "disappearances" reported. He would keep checking though.

To his rear, beyond the back door, the porch floorboard creaked. With his right hand he closed the scrapbook, while his left slipped down under the table and loosely took hold of the cricket bat. His muscles tensed, ready to use the back of his knees to send the chair crashing backwards into the doorway as he stood and turned.

No-one could sneak up on –

A clatter of claws. He turned to see Spotty licking his empty food bowl pathetically. It skittered around the kitchen floor under the persistent assault of Spotty's tongue. Chris relaxed. Everything was normal.

After locking up and putting the lights out he stripped and slipped back between the sheets as stealthily as he could, careful not to touch Rosa with his hands until they warmed up.

She murmured, "Bad dream again?"

"Yes. Just a dream. Go back to sleep," he whispered.

She pulled his arm round her waist and he snuggled up closer, smelling her hair, whatever it was she used on it: her body heat warmed him as his belly touched her back. Shared heat to drive out the cold.

She had taken him back, despite the way he had disappeared from her life while on the run. He was learning a lot about forgiveness by being with her. She was a better person than he was.

When he'd left her he had told himself he was running because of the law, that he'd had no choice. But why had he got involved with that job, at that time? As an *excuse*?

He had a lot of thinking to do.

But for now he could make amends, and stop being a dick.

He didn't really like the place she lived – out in the country, too isolated, *too many fucking woods*; but she loved it, and he was willing to make compromises.

Anyway, you have to face up to fears, not run from them.

This could be it for him. If he played his cards right, the two of them could make a real go of it. The phrase "everybody needs somebody" drifted through his sleepy head, a piece of advice he had taken to heart, the least he could do.

He would do his best not to Fuck It Up.

And if anyone tried to mess up his life now that he was determined to go straight, now that he had found somewhere safe ...

They'd be fucking sorry.

He kissed the back of Rosa's neck and went to sleep.

About The Author

Karl Drinkwater is an author with a silly name and a thousand-mile stare. He writes dystopian space opera, dark suspense and diverse social fiction. If you want compelling stories and characters worth caring about, then you're in the right place. Welcome!

Karl lives in Scotland and owns two kilts. He has degrees in librarianship, literature and classics, but also studied astronomy and philosophy. Dolly the cat helps him finish books by sleeping on his lap so he can't leave the desk. When he isn't writing he loves music, nature, games and vegan cake.

Go to karldrinkwater.uk to view all his books grouped by genre.

As well as crafting his own fictional worlds, Karl has supported other writers for years with his creative writing workshops, editorial services, articles on writing and publishing, and mentoring of new authors. He's also judged writing competitions such as the international Bram Stoker Awards, which act as a snapshot of quality contemporary fiction.

Don't Miss Out!

Enter your email at karldrinkwater.substack.com to be notified about his new books. Fans mean a lot to him, and replies to the newsletter go straight to his inbox, where every email is read. There is also an option for paid subscribers to support his work: in exchange you receive additional posts and complimentary books.

Other Titles

Lost Solace

Lost Solace

Chasing Solace

Hidden Solace

Raising Solace

Finding Solace

Lost Tales Of Solace

Helene

Grubane

Clarissa

Ruabon

UESI

Standalone Suspense

Turner

They Move Below

Harvest Festival

Manchester Summer

Cold Fusion 2000

2000 Tunes

Contemporary Short Stories

It Will Be Quick

Non-fiction

From Idea To Item

Collected Editions

Karl Drinkwater's Horror Collection

Lost Solace Five Book Edition

Author's Notes

Lord Richard Ap Celwyddau – the current Lord of Stawl Island – provided hospitality and information while I wrote Turner. This is a work of fiction but some of the background details *are* true. Firstly, Stawl Island was originally a home for piracy, which ended when the original Lord Weston was granted the island in the fifteenth century. Lord Weston stayed on the island for at least some of each year, as did his descendants.

In the early eighteenth century the thirteenth Lord Weston did a rare thing – he changed the family name. Not to the fictional Ynyr Fychan, but to Ap Celwyddau.

The only other true fact is the geology of the sandbar which sometimes connects Stawl Island to the mainland. The current Lord Ap Celwyddau informed the author that a few pedantic and judgementally rude writers about Ynys Diawl seem to enjoy debating whether it is really *Ynys* Diawl (Devil *Island*), or Diawl *Yno* (the Devil *over there*).

It should be added that the island has always been closed to tourists, but after reading the first draft of my novel Lord

Richard said he found the whole thing "rather amusing", and that he was willing to open up the island to visitors. "Who knows, it could lead to a gruesome sightseeing industry," he mused, "and there is no harm in occasionally muddying the waters, so to speak." The island's residents are preparing for the first visitors in the near future.

Thanks

I am very grateful for the help I received from Janet Thomas in improving the novel, despite the grim subject matter. I'm also grateful to Susan Walton for her additional help in removing my errors and to Elin Williams for correcting my Welsh. And, obviously, I owe a lot to my patron, Lord Richard Ap Celwyddau. Lastly, many thanks to Tom Freeman for his wonderfully spirited performance narrating the audiobook.

Printed at Repro India Ltd.